Bloom County Books by Berke Breathed

LOOSE TAILS

'TOONS FOR OUR TIMES

PENGUIN DREAMS and Stranger Things

BLOOM COUNTY BABYLON:
Five Years of Basic Naughtiness

MOM QUEST: Opus Goes Home
A Bloom County Calendar for 1988

and

BILLY AND THE BOINGERS BOOTLEG

BILLY
AND THE
BOINGERS
BOOTLEG

A Bloom County Book

Berke Breathed

Little, Brown and Company · Boston · Toronto

COPYRIGHT © 1987 BY THE WASHINGTON POST COMPANY

ALL RIGHTS RESERVED. NO PART OF THIS BOOK MAY BE REPRO-
DUCED IN ANY FORM OR BY ANY ELECTRONIC OR MECHANICAL
MEANS, INCLUDING INFORMATION STORAGE AND RETRIEVAL
SYSTEMS, WITHOUT PERMISSION IN WRITING FROM THE PUB-
LISHER, EXCEPT BY A REVIEWER WHO MAY QUOTE BRIEF PAS-
SAGES IN A REVIEW.

FIRST EDITION

LIBRARY OF CONGRESS CATALOG CARD NO.: 87-3537

Bloom County is syndicated by The Washington Post Writers Group.

"I'm a Boinger" and "U-Stink-But-I-♥-U" are reproduced on
imprint and record by permission of Berke Breathed. Copyright
© 1987 by Berke Breathed.

Published simultaneously in Canada
by Little, Brown & Company (Canada) Limited

PRINTED IN THE UNITED STATES OF AMERICA

I'M A BOINGER
(S. Dallas)

A bird on the bass
A tongue, what a face!
At best, the music could be described as lame

Sure we look disgusting
But whose chops are we busting
In a year, maybe two, we'll seem tame

And three years down the track
We'll be a Las Vegas lounge act
We'll be back
We'll be back, 'cus we're the Boingers

Jimmy dropped his pants
And Ozzy dines on bats
And Hendrix played guitar with his teeth

The Deadheads got their Jerry
And Mom's got her Barry
And Ronnie listens to guys like Falwell and Meese

But if you don't know by now
Bill bit the head off a cow
That's no lie
That's no lie, 'cus we're the Boingers

Was Bowie ever a fairy?
Was Debbie ever Harry?
Was Elvis ever the King? — let's not be reflective

Does Barbra wish she was a goy?
Is George really a boy?
Is Filthy ever Divine? — it's all subjective

Answers to all this
Lie with their psychoanalysts
Just relax
Just relax
I can't relax!
I can't relax, 'cus I'm a Boinger!

U-STINK-BUT-I-❤-U
(B. Catt)

I hate the way you act
And I hate the way you smell
I hate the way you look, girl,
'Cus you just look like hell

Chorus:
You make me sick! Way-oh, Way-oh, Way-oh
You make me sick! You really stink, girl
You make me sick! Way-oh, Way-oh, Way-oh
You make me sick!
(Tuba Solo)
. . . But I luuuuv you

I hate your polyester pantsuits
And your greasy hair,
And that stuff between your braces
And your hairy derriere

Chorus
(Guitar Solo)

When I got you in my backseat
And I tried to make my move
I had to roll down all the windows
To keep my face from turning blue

Chorus
(Tuba Solo)

THE BOINGERS are

**Steve Dallas — Guitars, Lead Vocalizin'
& Socializin'**
**Wild Bill Cat — Tongue Twangin' and
Head Bangin'**
**Opus Croakus — 'Lectric Tuba, Mouth
Harps & Sweethearts**
**Hodge-Podge — Skins, Squints &
Creme Rinse**

Additional Musicians:
THE HARRY PITTS BAND ("I'm a Boinger"):
by Richard LaClaire with Scott Freilich, Rick Kazmierczak,
Mike Brydalski

MUCKY PUP ("U-Stink-But-I-❤-U")
by Bill Casler with Chris Milnes, John Milnes, Danny Nastasi,
Scott Lepage

THANX TO: Milo B. (Don't worry, we'll re-plaster the basement . . . Awright!), Larry at Central leather and stud boutique, Esther at International Crabby Management (Kiss my principal tuckus, Victoria, eh?), Bill "Party Pony" Dickinson, Goober at Dino's Guitar Mart; also xtra freakin' yahooz to Don "Metalmaniac" Graham (Gummibears! Gummibears!), Lee "Clone Drone" Salem (We know wats in YER Anxiety closet!), Michael HoBO Fuchs (Bill ze Cat is comin to tinkle in yer dish!), Katie Mack . . . thanx fer the smiles and the groovy gams, babe. And thanks to the faithful Boingers Metalbashers who bought our last record. All 37 of you.
ROCK 'N' ROLL ROYALTIES FOREVER BABEEEE!

Due to the recent reruns, we have been asked to summarize the current story line as it was left six weeks ago... ahem...

official spokesperson

Cutter John, having been—

I..after having an affair with Madonna, am stalked by a rabid Sean Penn. Meanwhile, Steve Dallas is spotted playing leapfrog with a scantily clad Imelda Marcos.

official

Well, that's the sort of plot we **should** have. But don't mind me... please continue.

official spokesperson

The reruns, by the way, were a result of a catastrophic medical crisis within our "Bloom County" family.

Opus had nose hemorrhoids.

Lies!

official spokesperson

I shall now proceed with the "Bloom County" story update... unless "Mister Plot Revisionist" has any more comments.

I don't have to stand here and **take that!**

official spokesperson

"Cutter John, having been plucked from the Atlantic as a suspected spy, remains in the clutches of Soviet interrogators.

Six "Chicken McNuggets"... or I don't talk.

Nyet!

...while the traitorous **Bill the Cat** vegetates in a local prison calmly awaiting his imminent execution."

≈ Sigh ≈

Lake Siberia Days K. Marx

I ♥ Leningrad

That's it. And exciting stuff it is!

Anything to add?

Me? I read "Garfield."

Garfield Gets Old

Poor Bill the Cat... poor ol' doomed Bill the communist cat.

Milo's Meadow

S'pose there's any hope?

Steve Dallas is working hard to build public sympathy for a reprieve...

Milo's Meadow

In fact, he's going over last-minute strategy with Bill right now...

...and stop screaming out the prison window, "Ronald McDonald is a capitalist stooge"!!

Thpt. Bleck..

1

5

HOME!! HOME AT LAST!!

AIR BOLSHEVIK

POINK POINK

CAPTAIN!!

ESCAPED FROM THOSE ROMULAN HEATHENS, EH, CAPTAIN?

WE'LL BLAST 'EM WITH A PHOTON WHATZIMAJIGGER!!

AHOY. AHOY.

AHEAD WARP 37 TO THE WILD, LOUD PLANET OF LUSTY WOMEN COMMODI-TIES BROKERS!!

EVERY-THING'S BACK TO NORMAL!

SO TO SPEAK.

YESSIREE! SURE AM GLAD THEY TRANSFERRED ME OUT OF "PERSONALS"...

PHOTOGRAPHY Dept. "BLOOM BEACON"

HMM... NEWSPAPER PHOTOGRAPHER... MOSTLY TAKIN' PICTURES OF PIGEONS AND BABIES IN THE PARK, I SPECT...

HMM... SEDATE... SERENE... NO CONFRONTATION...

YOW! ..THIS IS MY TYPE OF JOB!!

SEAN PENN HAS BEEN SPOTTED NEARBY. GO SIC 'IM.

PHOTOGRAPHY Dept. "BLOOM BEACON"

SEAN PENN IS HERE?! IN TOWN?

HE'S DRINKING AT A LOCAL BAR.

GOSSIP LIES ER.

AND YOU SENT OPUS TO GET CANDID PHOTOS?!

RELAX. STEVE WENT ALONG.

GOSSIP LIES ER.

PENN WILL EAT THEM!!

MAYBE THEY'LL CATCH HIM IN A GOOD MOOD...

GOSSIP LIES ER.

HE'S THROWING UP IN THE ALLEY. BETTER USE A FLASH...

OH MY...

6

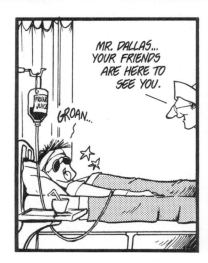

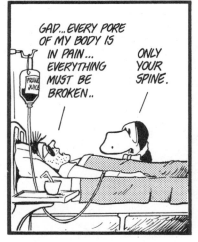

9

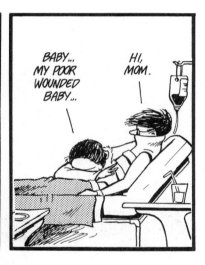

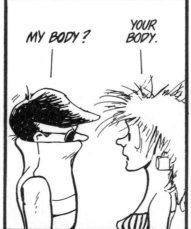

12

MAN OH MAN... I WISH THERE WAS A MILKSHAKE SITTIN' ON MY BELLY RIGHT NOW.

BLOOM COUNTY BACKSTAGE AREA NO GROUPIES

MR. OPUS

SO ASK FOR ONE. WE'RE IN THE FUNNIES... ANYTHING IS POSSIBLE IN THE FUNNIES.

AWRIGHT. I'D LIKE A WHOPPING BIG SARDINE AND BEER MILKSHAKE.

WHOA! THE COMIC WORLD REALLY **IS** A SEPARATE REALITY! I'D ALSO LIKE A PAIR OF RED SNEAKERS...

YOW! TOTALLY FAB! UH... NOW HOW 'BOUT A 200-POUND GREEN AND MAUVE DUCK SITTING ON MY HEAD...

WOW! THE PHILOSOPHICAL IMPLICATIONS ARE STAGGERING! IMAGINE! OKAY... WHAT NEXT...

I'M OUTTA HERE.

MR. BLOOM

...KATHLEEN SULLIVAN... IN SPANDEX... IN A HOT TUB... FILLED WITH WARM JELL-O...

SO SORRY. LAST PANEL.

MR. OPUS

STEVE'S LAW TIPS

NUMBER 29 "WHO SHOULD I SUE?"

GOOD MORNING. TODAY'S TIP IS ON EFFECTIVE SUING. LET'S LOOK AT MY OWN RECENT EXAMPLE...

ON APRIL 17TH, THE PLAINTIFF, ME, WAS BRUTALLY ATTACKED BY ACTOR SEAN PENN AFTER I ACCIDENTALLY AND NOT ON PURPOSE SNAPPED A PICTURE OF HIM.
THE QUESTION: WHO SHOULD I SUE?...

...SEAN?

NO. JURIES LOVE FAMOUS PEOPLE. PLUS, HE'D PROBABLY RETURN TO BEAT UP THE PLAINTIFF AGAIN. NEVER SUE PSYCHOPATHIC CELEBRITIES.

...SEAN'S WIFE?

NO. TRUE, LIVING WITH MADONNA MIGHT MAKE MOST ANYONE IRRITABLE, BUT PROVING LIABILITY WOULD BE DIFFICULT. PLUS, SHE TOO MIGHT RETURN TO BEAT UP THE PLAINTIFF.

...OPUS?

ME?!

..NO. ALTHOUGH HE GOT THE PLAINTIFF INTO THIS MESS, HE'S ALSO DEAD BROKE. NEVER, NEVER, NEVER SUE POOR PEOPLE.

...THE NIKOLTA CAMERA CO.?

NIKOLTA

YES! A MAJOR CORPORATION WITH GOBS OF LIQUID CASH, IT WAS CRIMINALLY NEGLIGENT IN NOT PUTTING STICKERS ON THEIR CAMERAS WHICH READ, "WARNING: PHYSICAL INJURY MAY RESULT FROM PHOTOGRAPHING PSYCHOPATHIC HOLLYWOOD HOTHEADS."

...I PLAN TO ASK FOR $10 MILLION...

AMERICA! LAND OF THE LAWSUIT!! GOD BLESS HER!!

IT'S A LETTER AND PHOTO FROM BILL THE CAT.

YEAH? FROM RUSSIA?

"HI, FELLAS. BEEN SUPER BUSY. ENCLOSED FIND PIC OF ME AT FIRST JOB IN THIS GLORIOUS WORKERS' PARADISE: CHIEF MANAGER OF THE CHERNOBYL NUCLEAR POWER PLANT..."

DANGER: DO NOT LEAN ON LEVER

"...AM NOW ON SECOND JOB."

GOOD HEAVENS.

WHERE'S MISTER SPOCK? WE HAVE A FIVE-YEAR MISSION TO GET CRACKIN' ON.

HE'S DAWDLING INSIDE STARBASE.

THAT STUPID VULCAN... WHAT'S HE DOING IN THERE?

I'LL TELL YA WHAT HE'S DOING...

..HE'S PROBABLY SHARPENING HIS EARS!!

NO, BUT HE IS POWDERING HIS NOSE, THANK YOU VERY MUCH.

CHIEF SCIENCE OFFICER SPOCK OF THE STARCHAIR "ENTERPOOP" PAUSES TO PONDER HIS PURPOSE:

MILO'S MEADOW STARBASE

TO EXPLORE STRANGE NEW WORLDS...TO SEEK OUT EXCITING NEW ALIEN LIFE FORMS...

...TO HAVE GRACE JONES DANCE "THE WATUSI" ON MY BACK IN STILETTO HEELS.

INDEED...TO GO WHERE NO MAN HAS GONE BEFORE..

BACK UP..

14

ADRIFT IN THE COSMOS... ENEMIES ALL AROUND... CREW MORALE DANGEROUSLY LOW...

ONLY ONE THING LEFT TO DO...

LET'S BLAST THE HOLY BEJEEZUS OUT OF THE SAVAGE DESERT PLANET LIBYA!

INSTANT GRATIFICATION: THE STUFF OF LEADERSHIP.

HEY SPOCK... PACKAGE FOR YOU FROM THE DEFENSE DEPARTMENT.

DEFENSE DEPARTMENT?

"TO MR. O. SPOCK, CHIEF SCIENCE OFFICER... 'STAR TREK' STRATEGIC DEFENSE PROJECT"

DON'T THEY MEAN "STAR WARS"?

IT'S DOUGH! GOBS AND GOBS OF DOUGH!

JUMPIN' JEHOSHAPHAT! THIS MEANS ONLY ONE THING...

THINGS IS GETTIN' A MITE CONFUSED DOWN WEINBERGER WAY!!

WHAT'S THIS?

MOOLAH. THE PENTAGON HAS APPARENTLY DECIDED THAT OPUS IS ONE "MR. SPOCK, CHIEF SCIENCE OFFICER FOR 'STAR TREK' STRATEGIC DEFENSE RESEARCH."

BOXES OF DOUGH HAVE BEEN ARRIVING FOR THREE DAYS.

761... 762...

YOU JEST.

SIR, I DO NOT.

773... 774... 775...

HOW MUCH?

$779 MILLION! ICE CREAM'S ON ME!

RRRING !!

OH, HI !.. YES.. FINE... WHAT ? A HAWAIIAN PARTY ? 500 GUESTS ? I'D LOVE TO !

I'LL FLY IN ON A PRIVATE JET TOMORROW... RIGHT... SEE YOU THERE... GIVE MY BEST TO YOUR ENTOURAGE..

..OH, AND GIVE IMELDA A SQUEEZE FOR ME ...

AWRIGHT.. THAT'S IT !!

I THINK WE'VE HAD JUST ABOUT ENOUGH OF YOU, MR. WALKING PENTAGON PORK-BARREL !!

STOP YELLING AT ME.

YOU'RE SPOILED.. YOU'RE BOORISH.. AND YOU'RE TOO RICH. I THINK YOU SHOULD GIVE EVERYTHING BACK.

I CAN'T DO THAT.

WHY NOT ?

I BOUGHT BOLIVIA.

DID YOU KEEP THE RECEIPT ?!

OO... HELLO, MACHO MAN !

HELLO, HELLO !

AND WHAT KIND OF EXCITEMENT DID YOU GET INTO RECENTLY ?

WELL ... SINCE YOU BROUGHT IT UP...

AS I WAS PULLING THIS SCREAMING WOMAN AWAY FROM 700 KLAN BIKER RAPISTS, I--

HE RAN INTO SEAN PENN'S FOREHEAD.

SO. YOU'RE LOOKING TO DIE EARLY, THEN ...

WELL, AT LEAST I'LL GO TO HEAVEN ...

WHO'S ON THE PHONE WITH OPUS? THE PENTAGON.

THEY ASKED TO SPEAK WITH CHIEF SCIENCE OFFICER **SPOCK** OF THE "STAR TREK SPACE DEFENSE RESEARCH TEAM"... WHO THEY'VE RECENTLY SENT $900 MILLION...

WHAT DO THEY WANT? TO SEE THE FINISHED PROJECT NEXT TUESDAY.

DR. SPOCK? HELLO?

MILO... THE PENTAGON WANTS TO SEE A WORKING SPACE-DEFENSE GIZMO BY TUESDAY... OR THEY CUT OFF THE FUNDING FOR OUR "STAR WARS" PROJECT!

OPUS... SNAP OUT OF IT... THERE IS NO-- CAN YOU IMAGINE? THE CUTTING OF **ANY** DEFENSE FUNDING?! THEY **MUST** KEEP THE MONEY COMING! LOTS OF IT! **UN**-LIMITED MONEY!

WHY, FER CRYIN' OUT LOUD.. RESEARCH PHYSICISTS NEED PORSCHES, TOO!!

SAD, BUT TRUE. MY GOD... THE DAYS OF WINE AND ROSES ARE OVER, AREN'T THEY?

OLIVER! WAKE UP! I NEED YOUR HELP!

I'VE RECEIVED $926 MILLION FROM UNCLE SAM AND NOW HE WANTS ME TO COUGH UP A WORKING "STAR WARS" SYSTEM BY TUESDAY!

PLEASE! HELP ME! I CAN PAY! I'M LOADED! I'LL MAKE YOU RICH! WHADDYA WANT? STOCKS? BONDS? PERSIAN RUGS?

A WAFFLE. WAFFLES! GOOD! HOW MANY? THIRTY MILLION? CORNER THE WAFFLE MARKET?

19

HI, MILO. WE'VE JUST GOTTEN INTO D.C. ... RIGHT... WE'LL BE MAKING OUR "STAR WARS" PRESENTATION TO CONGRESS TOMORROW..

WHAT'S THAT?... HOW WAS OUR FLIGHT?

WELL, THERE WAS SOME TURBULENCE...

MILO SAYS TO UNBUCKLE NOW.

NOPE NOPE NOPE NOPE NOPE NOPE NOPE NOPE...

BRUSH BRUSH BRUSH BRUSH BRUSH

A TIP: NEVER SHARE A HOTEL ROOM WITH A FLIGHTLESS WATERFOWL PREPARING FOR BED.

GARGLE GARGLE GARGLE GARGLE GARGLE

SPIT!

FINISHED?

NOPE. GOTTA FLOSS MY TOES.

GREAT... HERE WE ARE... ABOUT TO PRESENT A PERFECTLY RIDICULOUS "STAR WARS" DEFENSE PLAN TO THE U.S. CONGRESS... GAD!

...AND ALL AROUND US... OTHER BRILLIANT RESEARCH SCIENTISTS THE GOVERNMENT IS ALSO FUNDING.

WONDER WHAT THIS FELLOW IS WORKING ON?

SAY THERE... WHAT--

GIANT LASER SPACE FRISBEES.

DR. OPUS SPOCK... WE'VE SENT YOU $900 MILLION FOR RESEARCH. TELL US... IS A "STAR TREK" STRATEGIC DEFENSE PROJECT REALISTIC?

UH... SURE.

AND IT'LL PROTECT THIS COUNTRY FROM OVER 5000 ENEMY MISSILES?

UH.. SURE.

AMERICA CAN AFFORD IT?

UH.. SURE.

THANK YOU, SIR. WE APPRECIATE THE HONEST CANDOR OF GOVERNMENT-FUNDED SCIENTISTS LIKE YOURSELF.

NO SWEAT.

THUS, LADIES AND GENTLEMEN... OUR STRATEGIC DEFENSE PLAN:
(A) COLLECT $500 BILLION IN SMALL BILLS...

...(B) SEW BILLS INTO HUGE MISSILE NET CIRCLING GLOBE.

WELL... THAT'S IT. WHADDYA SAY? TOO GOOFY?

DID YOU BUY IT?

The Washington Post

THEY BOUGHT IT

$10 BILLION VOTED FOR FURTHER RESEARCH ON "NET WARS" DEFENSE PLAN

GENIUS?

WELL, DAD, I GUESS IT ISN'T NEWS TO YOU THAT "DYNASTY" STAR HEATHER LOCKLEAR MARRIED "MOTLEY CRÜE" DRUMMER TOMMY LEE LAST MONTH...

NOW, CAN'T YOU JUST IMAGINE WHAT THE SENIOR MRS. LOCKLEAR MUST HAVE THOUGHT UPON HEARING THAT HER DAUGHTER WAS TO WED A MAN WHO HAD THE WORD "HEATHER" TATTOOED ON EACH BUTTOCK?

REALLY. CAN'T YOU IMAGINE WHAT SHE THOUGHT? WELL, I'LL TELL YOU WHAT SHE THOUGHT...

AAAIIGH!!

SON...

Panel 1: WE INTERRUPT THE COMIC FOR A VITAL PUBLIC-SERVICE MESSAGE: IN AN EFFORT TO OFFSET THE ALARMING 13% DECREASE IN FREQUENCY OF **LEE IACOCCA'S** FACE ON TV, BOOKS AND MAGAZINES WITHIN THE LAST SIX DAYS, WE OFFER THE FOLLOWING:

MR. LIBERTY AT AGE 5

HIS IMMIGRANT MOTHER

Panel 3: IACOCCA: TOO MUCH IS NEVER ENOUGH.

WHEW! I WAS GOING INTO WITHDRAWAL...

Panel 4: AS A TRIBUTE TO LEE "MR. AMERICA" IACOCCA, WE HAVE A SPECIAL GUEST STAR...

"VALENTINE"... THE DANCING COCKROACH! TAKE IT AWAY!

AHEM..

A TRIBUTE

Panel 5: OH GIMME HYPE! PUBLICITY! GET DEM STRETCH MARKS OFF MISS LIBERTY! MOCHA! POLKA! PATRIOTIC TAPIOCA... DAT'S WHAT IS MY IACOCCA!

Panel 6: UNION BUSTING! PROFIT LUSTING! LITTLE PINTOS ALL COMBUSTING! APPLE PIE AND DIET COKE-A...! **DAT'S WHAT IS MY IACOCCA!!**

Panel 7: WELL! THAT WAS SIMPLY--

...AWFUL.

SHWAK!

A TRIBUTE

Panel 8: IT WAS A WARM JUNE DAY WHEN OPUS FINALLY HEARD THE NEWS.

WHAT NEWS?

Panel 9: ..THAT COLLEGE-EDUCATED PENGUINS WHO ARE STILL SINGLE AT AGE SIX HAVE ONLY A 3% CHANCE OF EVER GETTING MARRIED.

BUT **I'M** SIX!!

Panel 10: ...THIS CAN'T BE! THIS CAN'T BE!! I'LL DIE AN OLD WATERFOWL MAID!! OH, I WISH I HADN'T HEARD THIS!!

Panel 11: ANY REGRETS?

YEAH. I REGRET THIS WASN'T ANOTHER DUMB IACOCCA EPISODE.

23

HI.

HI. HI.

HOW ABOUT DROPPING YOUR CAREER, MARRYING ME, MOVING TO ANTARCTICA, RAISING TEN KIDS, AND LAVISHING ME WITH LOVE AND DEVOTION BETWEEN POKER GAMES THROUGHOUT MY OLD AGE?

FORGET IT.

DRAT! IT'S THE HAT, ISN'T IT?

AWRIGHT...FIRST LET'S FIGURE JUST WHAT SORT OF WOMAN IS YOUR IDEAL WIFE... GIMME SOME EXAMPLES.

JUNE LOCKHART IN "LASSIE".

WHO ELSE?

EDITH BUNKER... JANE WYATT IN "FATHER KNOWS BEST"! JUNE CLEAVER OF "LEAVE IT TO BEAVER"...

I SEE A TREND HERE...

BOY, JUNE SURE COULD PUSH A MEAN MOP...

"SLAVE"...

THEN, OF COURSE, THERE'S MISS FEBRUARY...

FORM FOR PERSONAL AD: Print neatly..

"TALL, SEXY, HANDSOME, SVELTE, ATHLETIC, MUSCLED, PETITE-NOSED SEXUAL POWERHOUSE OF A DUDE SEEKS GAL FOR WIFE".

OH, AND I SUPPOSE YOU ALL DON'T FIB A LITTLE ON YOUR INCOME TAX?

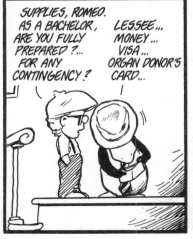

25

HELLO! YOU'RE THE LADY WHO CALLED ABOUT MY PERSONAL AD?

YES. AND YOU'RE THE TALL, SVELTE, MUSCLED TOWER OF VIRILITY IT DESCRIBED?

YUP. SAY, THAT'S A REAL HEAD OF HAIR ON THOSE LEGS.. SO TO SPEAK.

THANKS. YOUR NAME IS...?

OPUS. AND YOU ARE...?

LOLA GRANOLA

OF COURSE YOU ARE.

WELL, MISS LOLA GRANOLA... NOW THAT WE'VE INTRODUCED OURSELVES, LET'S SKEEDADDLE ON TO THE RESTAURANT. TALLY-HO!!

UH.. I'LL BE AT THE CAR IN A MINUTE, LOLA... I'VE LEFT SOME UNFINISHED BUSINESS...

JUST THIS ONCE I'D LIKE TO BE ABLE TO GO OUT WITH A WOMAN AND POSSIBLE FUTURE WIFE WITHOUT ALL OF YOU TAGGING ALONG THANK YOU VERY MUCH!

CLICK!

WE INTERRUPT THE STORY TO READ A LETTER FROM THE EDWIN MEESE COMMISSION ON PORNOGRAPHY THAT WAS SENT TO ALL SIX AMERICAN NEWSPAPERS WHICH CARRY "BLOOM COUNTY."

"DEAR NEWSPAPER EDITOR, WE HAVE RECEIVED TESTIMONY THAT YOUR COMIC PAGE INCLUDES A FEATURE WHICH FREQUENTLY MAKES USE OF THE 14-LETTER 'S' WORD..."

"THE 'S' WORD"?

"THE MEESE COMMISSION HAS DETERMINED A CAUSAL RELATIONSHIP BETWEEN THE USE OF THE 'S' WORD AND THE RECENT INCREASE IN MURDER, UNCLE ABUSE AND DOG HICKEYS."

"THE 'S' WORD"?

LADIES AND GENTLEMEN... I FEAR THEY ARE SPEAKING OF US.

"SNUGGLE-BUNNIES"?

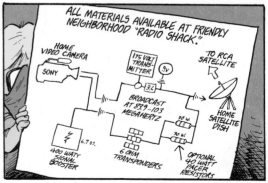

SNIFF

SNIFF
SNIFF

CHOMP

ALERT!! THE RUMOR REGARDING THE EFFECTS OF DANDELION CONSUMPTION IS NOT, REPEAT, **NOT**, JUST ANOTHER RECKLESS FABRICATION OF AN INCREASINGLY SENSATIONALISTIC AND LIBERAL-LEANING MEDIA ESTABLISHMENT!

AND WHY THE HELL SHOULDN'T I EAT A STUPID DANDELION, BLOB-BUTT?

YOU DON'T KNOW?

DON'T EAT THE DANDELIONS

WHY, BECAUSE FROM PERSONAL EXPERIENCE I KNOW THAT THE EATING OF DANDELIONS WILL RESULT IN A SUDDEN PHYSICAL TRANSFORMATION INTO THE MOST SHOCKING, PUREST FORM OF ONE'S TRUE INNER ESSENCE!

DON'T EAT TH' DANDELIONS

MY INNER ESSENCE, EH? I'LL TRY ONE.

NO!!

CHOMP!

THERE ARE THINGS MAN WAS JUST NEVER MEANT TO KNOW ABOUT HIMSELF!

AARGH!

OH GOD, HELP HIM!!

THIS, ACTUALLY, COMES AS A SURPRISE TO NO ONE.

SPAM

33

OH, SWEET WOOGUMS! BIG DADDY IS HERE!

I'M IN MY STUDIO!

THAT'S MY FIANCÉE, LOLA GRANOLA. SHE'S A SERIOUS MODERN ARTIST WHO'S WORKING ON A COMMISSION BY THE CITY COUNCIL TO CREATE A CONTEMPORARY, TOTALLY 80'S STATUE OF LIBERTY FOR THE COURTHOUSE LAWN.

HOW'S IT GOING IN THERE, MY LITTLE RAUSCHENBERG?

TERRIBLE! IT JUST WON'T... IT ISN'T... IT...

..WELL, IT DOESN'T SOAR, DARN IT!!

OPUS... I INVITED MY OLD FRIEND BART TO HAVE DINNER WITH US TONIGHT.

WHADDYA MEAN "OLD FRIEND"?

OKAY...A FORMER LOVER.

WE'RE GOING TO DINE WITH YOUR EX-BOYFRIEND?

HE'S JUST A GOOD FRIEND. KEEP AN OPEN MIND.

THIS IS AWFUL... THIS IS A SOCIAL DISASTER!!

HEY... I CAN THINK OF WORSE PEOPLE TO BE COMING OVER FOR AN EVENING...

WHO? HITLER? CANNIBALS? 300 ELVIS IMPERSONATORS?

MILO! IT'S ME! LOLA'S INVITED SOME EX-FLAME OF HERS NAMED BART OVER FOR DINNER!

NOW JUST RELAX...

HEY! I CAN'T COMPETE WITH A "BART"! MAYBE A "DOUGLAS" OR A "ROGER"... BUT NOT A "BART"! JUST LISTEN TO IT... "BART, BART, BART, BART, BART..." YECH!

WHAT'S HIS LAST NAME?

SAY, LOLA... WHAT'S THIS GUY'S LAST NAME?

"SAVAGEWOOD."

DID YA HEAR THAT? I'M UP AGAINST BART SAVAGEWOOFER

"TAKE A VALIUM!"

LOLA, I HAVE SOMETHING TO SAY AND I BETTER JUST SAY IT BEFORE I DECIDE NOT TO SAY IT...

LOLA, I DON'T THINK IT'S FAIR TO ME, YOUR SWEET PATOOTIE, WHEN YOU CONTINUE TO ASSOCIATE WITH FORMER FLAMES...

THEREFORE, I MUST INSIST THAT YOU REFRAIN FROM EVER TALKING TO ANOTHER MAN AS LONG AS I'M ALIVE.

OPUS, YOU'RE SO CUTE WHEN YOU'RE NEANDERTHAL.

DON'T TRY TO BUTTER ME UP.

AH, HOW MY HEART DOTH ACHE FOR FARAWAY KINGDOMS IN FARAWAY LANDS...

WITH PALACES AND CARRIAGES AND BRAVE KINGS AND FAIR QUEENS...

AND KINGS-TO-BE AND SONS OF KINGS-TO-BE...

NO, WE SHALL NOT BE TELLING THE ROYAL NAVY TO "TAKE BACK" MASSACHUSETTS TODAY, SON.

MUM'S RIGHT. YER SUCH A BLOODY WIMP, DAD.

SO... WE'RE OFF FOR A ROYAL FAMILY OUTING, EH, MUM ?

HOPE WE GET TO SEE UNCLE ANDREW ! I LIKE UNCLE ANDREW'S STYLE...

RANDY ANDY ! RANDY ANDY ! RANDY ANDY ! RANDY ANDY !

TIME TO GO. FETCH YOUR FATHER.

HEY GNARLY CHARLIE !!

41

TODAY:

Bloom County Viewpoint ®

" THE READER'S
CHANCE TO
TALK BACK "

RECENTLY, THE EDITORS
OF THIS FEATURE RECEIVED
NUMEROUS COMPLAINTS
REGARDING LAST WEEK'S
EPISODES DEALING WITH
THE VITAL ISSUES SURROUNDING
THE BRITISH MONARCHY.

A REPRESENTATIVE
EXCERPT FOLLOWS :

→

I SAY, SON...
YOU'VE BOPPED
THE QUEEN MUM
ON THE NOODLE.

I WAS
AIMING
FOR AUNT
FERGIE'S
HIPS. CAN'T
SEE HOW I
BLOODY WELL
MISSED 'EM.

WE PROMISE AN OPPORTUNITY
FOR ANY RESPONSIBLE READERS
TO RESPOND... AND THEREFORE
WE REQUEST THAT ONE
SIR RUMWALD EDWARD
CHARLES CHATSFIELD III
OF THE TOLEDO CHAPTER
OF THE "FRIENDS OF ENGLAND"
PLEASE STOP CALLING OUR
OFFICES AND WAFFLING
INTO THE DARN PHONE.

— ed.

Bloom County Viewpoint ®

TODAY... A READER
RESPONDS TO LAST WEEK'S
CONTROVERSIAL EPISODES
WHICH DEALT SENSITIVELY
WITH TROUBLED AREAS WITHIN
THE BRITISH MONARCHY.

A TYPICAL EXCERPT
FOLLOWS :

→

TIME TO GO.
FETCH YOUR FATHER.

HEY
GNARLY
CHARLIE.!!

A CONCERNED READER...
CHOSEN AT RANDOM...
FOLLOWS WITH HIS
COMMENTS :

(HIS IDENTITY HAS
BEEN HIDDEN BECAUSE
OF POSSIBLE
COMMUNITY
RETRIBUTION...)

→

THIS SORT OF "HUMOR"
IS SIMPLY DISGRACEFUL.
WHY DON'T WE SEE MORE
"FAMILY" HUMOR ON THE
COMIC PAGE LIKE "NANCY"
OR "DOONESBURY" ?!

...AND FRANKLY, I THINK THAT
COMIC STRIPS LIKE THIS
ONE REPRESENT SECULAR
HUMANISM'S FIFTH COLUMN..
SNEAKING IN AND WARPING
THE MINDS OF OUR YOUTH
WITH--

...HEY !
WHO TURNED
ON THE LIGHTS ?

UH...
HA ! HA !
OOPS !...
GOTTA GO !...
LATE DATE !
BYE !

THANK YOU FOR WATCHING
"*Bloom County* Viewpoint"...

...THE OPPORTUNITY WE GIVE
YOU, THE READER, TO RESPOND
TO OPINIONS EXPRESSED IN
THIS FEATURE.

JOIN US WHEN WE PRESENT
THE SECOND INSTALLMENT
OF "VIEWPOINT" AT ABOUT
THE SAME TIME HELL
FREEZES OVER.

43

44

STEP FOUR: "FACING THE HORROR OF WITNESSING YOUR COMIC STRIP READ BEFORE PUBLICATION"

LET ME READ IT.

PRESS ROOM →

NO TIME! NO TIME!

DON'T YOU WANT AN OPINION?

NO! I HAVEN'T TIME TO DO IT OVER! I DON'T WANT TO HEAR!

I'LL JUST CHECK THE SPELLING...

ME EARS ARE CLOSED... MY EARS ARE CLOSED...

I DON'T GET IT.

AAIGH!

NOPE. I DON'T GET IT.

OH, COME ON! READ IT AGAIN!

SEE... IT'S A COMIC ALLEGORY ON THE FUTILITY OF UNREQUITED LOVE... I THINK THE WRY PUNCH LINE SUMS IT UP, DON'T YOU?

WELL, DON'T YOU GET IT? IS IT EVEN MODERATELY AMUSING?

IS THIS A TARANTULA?

IT'S A HOUSE.. JUST GIVE IT HERE..

FINAL STEP: "RELISH THE THRILL OF FINALLY DISCOVERING ONE'S COMIC STRIP REPRODUCED ON A TYPICAL, AVERAGE AMERICAN NEWSPAPER'S TYPICAL, AVERAGE COMIC PAGE.."

FLIP FLIP FLIP FLIP

HMM.

Funnies ↓

UH... HERE IT IS! NO.... NO, WAIT... IT'S JUST A TIRE AD... ..—THERE IT IS! NO... NO, IT'S JUST AN INK SMUDGE...

YEEEEAAH!

YEAH!! YEAH! YEAH! YEAH!

OO! OO! OO! OO! OO! OO! OO!

THPTF! THPTTP! THPTH.!!

ROCK! ROCK! ROLL! ROLL! ROCK! ROLL

UH-OH.

CLAP! CLAP! CLAP! CLAP! CLAP! CLAP! CLAP! CLAP! CLAP! CLAP! MORE!

DISCOVERED AT LAST... THE FAMOUS ROCK 'N' ROLL AIR GUITARIST SLUMPS TO THE STAGE...HIS AIR GUITAR SPRAWLED ACROSS HIS CHEST. HE IS FATALLY EMBARRASSED.

SHOULD I LET THE AIR GROUPIES IN NOW?

WE'RE THE CREW OF THE STARCHAIR "ENTERPOOP" AND THE OFFICIAL BIRTHDAY COMMITTEE OF MILO'S MEADOW... AND WE'RE HERE TO BUY OUR GOOD FRIEND AND CAPTAIN, CUTTER JOHN, SOME NEW WHEELS!

HONEST SAM'S WHEELCHAIRS

SOMETHING SPECIAL AND DIFFERENT, PLEASE... DISTINCTIVE BUT NOT OVERBEARING... SINGULARLY UNORTHODOX WITH JUST A TAD OF FLASH! LIKE HIM!

LET ME SHOW YOU OUR TOP MODEL!

WHAT'S SO DISTINCTIVE ABOUT THIS?

MAUVE ARMRESTS!

DO MAUVE ARMRESTS MAKE A SUITABLE "PERSONAL STATEMENT"?

CERTAINLY NOT.

READ OUR LIPS... WE WANT SOMETHING DIFFERENT.!!

GENTLEMEN... A WHEELCHAIR IS NOT A VEHICLE FOR PERSONAL EXPRESSION!! PERIOD.!!

SO HOW DO YA LIKE IT?

THE PHOTON TORPEDOES ARE UNDER THE REFRIGERATOR.

WE MADE IT... DID YA GUESS?

EVEN NOW, AS THE MEADOW SOCIETY WELCOMES BACK BILL THE CAT, SOMETHING IS GOING ON IN OLIVER W. JONES'S BASEMENT LABORATORY...SOMETHING THAT WILL FOREVER CHANGE THE RELATIONSHIP BETWEEN MAN AND HIS UNIVERSE...

YES...YOU ALL GUESSED IT... **TELEPORTATION!** AND AT THIS VERY MOMENT, OLIVER IS GOING TO TELEPORT HIS MOLECULES RIGHT THROUGH THE BASEMENT CEILING AND REARRANGE THEM HERE AT THE TOP OF THE STAIRS...

SHHKKK!!

APPARENTLY THTILL A FEW BUGTH IN THE THYTHTEM...

TELEPORTATION, EH SON? WHAT'S THAT?

WELL, PUTTING IT SIMPLY...

Telepor Booth

WE'LL BE ABLE TO INSTANTLY SEND ANYTHING ANYWHERE.

SO...LIKE, COULD YOU PUT MY SLIPPERS INTO A CLOSET IN EGYPT?

SURE.

Telepor Booth

COULD YOU PUT GEORGE BUSH INTO THE WHITE HOUSE?

OH, WHY DO YOU ALWAYS EXPECT THE IMPOSSIBLE FROM ME?!

Telepo Booth

HELLO, JONES. YOUR LAWN'S LOOKING GOOD.

THANKS, RUTHERFORD. YOURS TOO.

I'LL GET TO THE POINT. IT'S YOUR BOY AGAIN.

REALLY.

HE TELEPORTED 300 GUINEA PIGS INTO MY WIFE'S BATH THIS MORNING. SOMETHING'S GOT TO BE DONE, JONES.

LIKE WHAT?

THE NEIGHBORHOOD HAS BEEN CONSIDERING A GRENADE THROUGH YOUR WINDOW.

YOU WANNA SEE MY LEAVES DUMPED IN YOUR YARD AGAIN THIS YEAR, RUTHERFORD?

50

51

HERE IS THE OFFICE OF THE NEW CARTOONIST OF "THE BLOOM PICAYUNE." HIS NEW COMIC STRIP STARTED TODAY...

BROOM CLOSET

OFFICIAL Stripper

UNFORTUNATELY, TODAY'S STRIP INCLUDED THE WORD "DRIT"... WHICH MANY CARTOONISTS DON'T REALIZE IS A RACIAL SLUR TO MOST TAHITIANS.

BROOM CLOSET

OFFICIAL Stripper

THE "TAHITIAN DEFENSE LEAGUE" IS OUTSIDE THE BUILDING PICKETING AND GETTING RILED UP. ONE MIGHT WONDER WHETHER THE CARTOONIST IS AWARE OF THIS.

BROOM CLOSET

OFFICIAL Stripper

...AGAIN, ONE MIGHT WONDER WHETHER THE CARTOONIST—

BROOM CLOSET

HE IS AND A STATEMENT IS BEING PREPARED.

OFFICIAL Stripper

TELL THEM I'M INDISPOSED.

YOU TELL THEM. YOU DREW THE CARTOON.

I DIDN'T MEAN TO INSULT THEM WITH A RACIAL SLUR.

THEY'RE THE AMERICAN READING PUBLIC... THEY'RE VERY FORGIVING.

THEY'RE HAVING A CAMP FIRE!

THEY'RE BURNING YOU IN EFFIGY.

GET BACK OUT THERE!!

I'M VERY INDISPOSED.

MILO...I DON'T LIKE THE EXPRESSION ON YOUR FACE...

UH... THE LAWYERS WOULD LIKE TO DISCUSS THE CARTOON YOU SUBMITTED FOR TOMORROW.

OFFICIAL BLOOM PICAYUNE STRIPPER AT WORK

LAWYERS?.. NOT THE LAWYERS!! PLEASE, GOD, NOT THE LAWYERS!

YEEK!

—LEGAL DEPT.— ABANDON ALL HOPE YE WHO ENTER HERE

Panel 1: THE BLOOM PICAYUNE LEGAL DEPT. / UH... YOU CALLED, YOUR ROYAL LAWYERSHIPS?

Panel 2: YES. APPARENTLY, YOUR CARTOON REFERS TO TED KOPPEL WEARING WOMEN'S UNDERWEAR. / IT WAS A LITTLE JOKE. / PLEASE DO NOT FEED THE LAWYERS RAW MEAT

Panel 3: WE WOULDN'T WANT TO UPSET MR. KOPPEL INTO A LAWSUIT, WOULD WE? FORK IT OVER. / UH... / PLEASE NOT FEED LAWYERS RAW M...

Panel 4: WE'LL JUST CLEAN IT UP A LITTLE. / YOU'RE DRIPPING SLIME ON IT. / P... NO L... -RA...

Panel 5: WHAT HAPPENED? / THE LAWYERS "CLEANED UP" MY CARTOON.

Panel 6: I'M AFRAID IT HAD BEEN... A GOOD JOKE...

Panel 7: YES... A GOOD AND FUNNY JOKE. / A POTENTIAL GIGGLE CUT DOWN IN IT'S PRIME.

Panel 8: A GOOD, FUNNY AND DEAD JOKE. / OH, WHIMSICAL NOTION, WE HARDLY KNEW YE.

Panel 9: WELL, TERRORISM IS UP... THE ECONOMY IS DOWN... AND DAVID LETTERMAN'S FRONT TEETH ARE STILL SPREADING APART... WANNA KNOW WHAT I THINK?

Panel 10: I KNOW WHAT YOU THINK! YOU THINK NOTHING'S BEEN THE SAME SINCE MARIE OSMOND'S DIVORCE!! THAT'S ALWAYS WHAT YOU THINK!!

Panel 11: HOW PERFECTLY POOPY OF YOU TO SAY THAT. IN FACT, THIS WHOLE TOWN HAS BEEN ACTING POOPY LATELY.

Panel 12: IN FACT, THE WHOLE COUNTRY HAS GONE TO HELL IN A HANDBASKET SINCE DAVID LEE ROTH LEFT "VAN HALEN."

55

HERE IS THE INTREPID REPORTER FOR "THE BLOOM PICAYUNE" ON THE TRACK OF THE BIGGEST STORY OF HIS CAREER ...

MILO'S WOODS DEAD AHEAD

..THE SEARCH FOR THE FABLED **BASSELOPE**! SIR... WHAT, EXACTLY, IS A BASSELOPE?

PART BASSET HOUND... PART ANTELOPE. VERY RARE.

A BASSELOPE SOUNDS VICIOUS. HAVE ANY PROTECTION?

BRINGING UP THE REAR.

THE SHOES ARE BY "REEBOK"... THE WEAPON, BY "LOUISVILLE SLUGGER"...THE FASHIONS BY "BANANA REPUBLIC."
THANK YOU ALL SO MUCH!

YES, A BASSELOPE IS PART BASSET HOUND, PART ANTELOPE. THE MILITARY HAS BEEN LOOKING FOR ONE FOR YEARS ...

APPARENTLY, THEY WANT TO USE THEM AS...UH... SAY...WHERE ARE YOUR NEW "BANANA REPUBLIC" CLOTHES?

TOOK 'EM OFF.

DO YOU HAVE ANY IDEA WHAT HAPPENS WHEN YOU HIKE UP A PAIR OF SHORTS AND YOUR LEGS ARE ONLY TWO INCHES LONG?

NO.

THE EXPRESSION IS CALLED "GETTING A WEDGIE," BUT I SHAN'T ELABORATE.

QUIETLY, THE INTREPID REPORTER AND HIS ARMED ASSISTANT LIE IN WAIT FOR THEIR ELUSIVE PREY: THE FABLED **BASSELOPE**..

...SUDDENLY, THEY SPY THE RARE ANIMAL SCURRYING DEEP INTO THE INKY DARKNESS OF THE THICK WOODS! **THE CHASE IS ON!!**

SNIFF..

..RECKLESSLY, THEY TEAR THROUGH THE THORNS AND POISON IVY! AND TOGETHER THEY LEAP UPON THE BUCKING, SNORTING, SPITTING BEAST!!...

..FANGS GLISTEN! BLOOD FLOWS!...

FEEL PARTICULARLY COMPELLED TO KEEP UP WITH THIS STORY?

NOPE.

DOES OPUS STILL THINK HE'S THE LATE MARLIN PERKINS?

I DON'T THINK SO...

YES, I THINK HE'S SNAPPING OUT OF IT.

THEY WANT ME TO WRESTLE WITH A TWENTY-FOOT ANACONDA!! PLEASE... TELL MUTUAL OF OMAHA "NO CAN DO!"

GET ME A BUCKET OF ICE WATER.

I'M 103 YEARS OLD... I HATE SNAKES!

The Bloom Picayune   SCOOP!!

WORLD'S LAST BASSELOPE FOUND

FIRST BLURRY PHOTO

FOUND

"I SAW HIM PERSONALLY SLAUGHTER 63 WOMBATS AND DEVOUR A RHINOCEROS FOR BREAKFAST" REPORTS ACE REPORTER MILO BLOOM...

...MILO BLOOM...

When asked if the beast might not appreciate all this publicity, Bloom said that while basselopes might eat rhinoceroses... they

...they certainly don't read newspapers.

SO.. WORD WAS OUT... THE LAST BASSELOPE HAD BEEN FOUND. AND AMERICA'S ARMED FORCES MOBILIZED... LIKE THE ARMY...

THERE HE IS! SHOOT!

RUMMBBLE...

AND THE SPORTSMEN...

THERE HE IS! SHOOT!!

RUMMBBLE...

.., AND THE PRESS.

SHOOT! SHOOT!

RRUMMBBLLE...

REACTION WAS SWIFT ...

IT'S THE MEDIA!! DUCK!!

58

"..SO WE'LL BE SIGNING THE CONTRACTS TOMORROW. MY WORD.

"..A MERCHANDISING DEAL TO PRODUCE PLUSH TOY BASSELOPES...

SOON I'LL BE SEEING THOUSANDS OF LITTLE STUFFED ME ALL OVER SHOPPING MALLS AROUND THE COUNTRY...

I'D PREFER TO BE PULLED OVER CARPET TACKS AND DIPPED IN RUBBING ALCOHOL. IT'S NOT SO BAD. TRUST ME.

SON, WE WANT TO SEE THIS BASSELOPE THING. NOW. WHAT FOR? BASSELOPE REFUGE BUG OFF

A SMALL TACTICAL WARHEAD WOULD FIT NEATLY BETWEEN HIS ANTLERS. IT COULD BE THE "MX" DEPLOYMENT SYSTEM WE'VE BEEN LOOKING FOR.

THE REDS ARE RUMORED TO HAVE A BASSELOPE. OUR SIDE HAS NONE. DO YOU KNOW WHAT THAT MEANS, BOY?

A BASSELOPE GAP!! WAP! WAP! WAP!

I'M SORRY, ROSEBUD... I TRIED KEEPING HIM-- MAKE WAY! GENERAL DINK COMING THROUGH!

BIG FELLER, HOW WOULD YOU LIKE TO HELP OUT THE CAUSE OF FREEDOM AND AMERICAN FOREIGN POLICY?

HOW? RUN BEHIND ENEMY LINES WITH A TEN-MEGATON BOMB STRAPPED TO YOUR NOGGIN!

DAMMIT, CORPORAL, THE LITTLE BUGGER TINKLED ON MY "TONY LAMA'S". MUST'VE BEEN A DEMOCRAT, SIR.

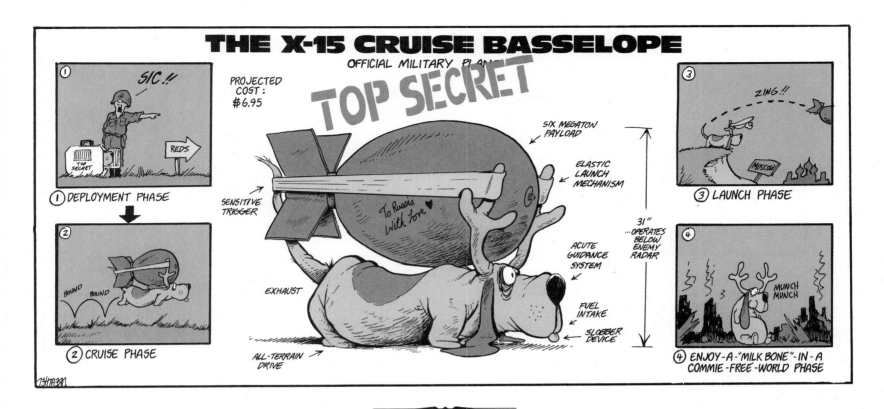

THE X-15 CRUISE BASSELOPE

OFFICIAL MILITARY PLAN

TOP SECRET

DAD! I DREAMT THAT MICHAEL JACKSON SLEEPS ON A BED OF PASTEURIZED PIG FAT TO KEEP HIS SKIN SOFT AND SUPPLE!! TELL ME IT AIN'T TRUE, DAD!

SON, THE TRUTH IS THAT HE SLEEPS IN A SPECIAL HIGH-PRESSURE OXYGEN CHAMBER TO MAKE HIM FEEL "REJUVENATED." I READ IT IN "NEWSWEEK".

REALLY.

WHEN THE GREAT GLOVED ONE GETS WEIRDER THAN MY NIGHTMARES, I KNOW WE'RE BOTH IN BIG, BIG TROUBLE.

HELLO? OH! LOLA! HELLO, MY LITTLE PERSIMMON! YES, I'VE MISSED YOU, TOO!

WHAT'S THAT? ME? MEET YOUR PARENTS FOR THE FIRST TIME? TOMORROW? DINNER? AT YOUR PLACE? UH...ER...

NO..I AM ENTHUSIASTIC! WHY, THERE'S NOTHING... NO, NOTHING I'D FIND PREFERABLE TO SPENDING AN EVENING WITH YOUR PARENTS TO GAIN THEIR APPROVAL!! NOTHING! NOTHING! RIGHT... GOODBYE.

NOTHING?

WELL. MAYBE GETTING DISSECTED AND PICKLED ALIVE BY ALIENS.

WAIT...LET US GUESS... YOU'RE GETTING CLEANED UP TO MEET YOUR FUTURE IN-LAWS AND YOU'RE A LITTLE NERVOUS.

I'M NOT A LITTLE NERVOUS.

WHY, I'LL JUST DAB A LITTLE "LISTERINE" TO THE OL' PITS...

SPLASH!

...AND FRESHEN THE BREATH WITH "RIGHT GUARD"! YEAH, I'M READY TO FACE ANYTHING!!

FOOOSH!!

...YOU'RE A LITTLE NERVOUS.

I'M A LITTLE NERVOUS.

Strip 1 — Row 1

Panel 1: DURING THE MILLENNIA THAT MEN AND FOWL HAVE SOUGHT AND SNARED WIVES...

PLOD PLOD

Panel 2: —SPEAKING OF WIFE-SNARING...WE INTERRUPT THE STORY FOR A SPECIAL "BINKLEY BULLETIN":

EXOTIC SINGER **MARIE OSMOND** WILL, REPEAT, <u>WILL</u> BE MARRYING AGAIN.

Panel 3: OUR SOURCES REPORT THAT LUCKY HUSBAND #2 IS GEORGE "MR. SULU" TAKEI OF "STAR TREK" FAME.

WE NOW RETURN TO THE STORY IN PROGRESS...

Panel 4: DURING THE MILLENNIA THAT MEN AND FOW... AND SNARED **FORGET IT. START OVER TOMORROW!**

Strip 2 — Row 2

Panel 1: DURING THE MILLENNIA THAT MEN AND FOWL HAVE SOUGHT AND SNARED WIVES...

PLOD PLOD

Panel 2: —HOLD IT! WE AGAIN INTERRUPT FOR A SPECIAL "BINKLEY BULLETIN CORRECTION":

DUE TO A TYPOGRAPHICAL ERROR, YESTERDAY WE MISTAKENLY REPORTED THAT MARIE OSMOND PLANNED TO WED GEORGE "MR. SULU" TAKEI.

WE'RE TERRIBLY EMBARRASSED...

Panel 3: IN REALITY, MS. OSMOND WILL BE MARRYING MR. OLAF BRIGHAM GIBSON, 67, OF MORMON FLATS, UTAH. SHE'LL BE MOVING IN WITH HIS 139 WIVES.

WE NOW RETURN TO THE STORY IN PROGRESS...

Panel 4: **THIS ?!... THIS..THIS PULP IS WHAT YOU INTERRUPT MY STORY FOR?**

DON'T GET RADICAL. WE GO TOMORROW.

Strip 3 — Row 3

Panel 1: DURING THE MILLENNIA THAT MEN AND FOWL HAVE SOUGHT AND SNARED WIVES, A TEST OF THEIR WORTHINESS HAS COME TO BE EXPECTED...

PLOD PLOD

Panel 2: ...A FORM OF QUALITY CONTROL... AS ONE WOULD SNIFF DUBIOUS FISH BEFORE ADDING IT TO THE SOUP.

LOLA GRANOLA

Panel 3: AND AS PRIMITIVE MAN MIGHT ONCE HAVE FACED A SLOBBERING SABER-TOOTHED TIGER TO PROVE HIS CHARACTER...

Panel 4: ...SO, TOO, DOES MODERN MAN GO TO FACE HIS FUTURE IN-LAWS.

I BROUGHT ALONG A CYANIDE SUICIDE PILL. YOU NEVER KNOW...

OPUS! FUTURE SON-IN-LAW..!!

GREETINGS AND SALUTATIONS, MR. GRANOLA.

ALWAYS HAPPY TO HAVE ANOTHER ★∂#!! MALE IN THIS ★#∂※ FAMILY!!

SAY.. HOW 'BOUT YOU AND ME CATCH SOME BALL GAMES... DRINK A FEW BREWS... SCREAM A FEW VULGARITIES AT WOMEN...

BETTER YET.. LET'S GO SHOOT A LARGE WILD ANIMAL AND EAT IT.

★∂#※ YEAH..

YEEK.

DON'T SAY IT, MOTHER.

FOR GOD'S SAKE, LOLA, WHY A PENGUIN?

BECAUSE, AT AGE 25, I'VE DETERMINED MEN ARE JERKS.

HONEY... YOU KNOW THERE'S SOMEBODY BETTER THAN A....A PENGUIN. HOW ABOUT THAT TOLEDO BOY?

TOLEDO..?

OH, YOU KNOW... THE BOY WITH THE HAIR.

ZOOEY... THE DRUMMER FOR "THE SCUM MONKEYS"?

YES. HOW ABOUT HIM?

OPUS? YOU IN THERE?

COMING, MY LITTLE TURTLE POOP!

WE'RE HAVING A FEW BEERTH AND WATCHING THOME WONDERFUL TV THPORTS PROGRAMTH.

YOU'RE DRUNK.

I....AM UNDERGOING "MALE BONDING" WITH YOUR FATHER.

BURP!

DADDY!!

...APPARENTLY, IT INVOLVES REPEATED VOMITING!

66

68

MEANWHILE... STEVE DALLAS'S LEGAL CAREER HAS SPED SMOOTHLY ALONG...

...AND THAT, GOOD FOLKS, IS WHY YOU SHOULD FIND MY CLIENT INNOCENT OF KILLING HIS TAX AUDITOR.

AND AS THE DEFENDANT, LET ME ADD ANOTHER REASON...

IF YA DON'T, I'LL STRANGLE YA.. I'LL HUNT DOWN YOUR RELATIVES AND SQUASH 'EM!! I'LL SHAVE YOUR CATS!!

CLEARLY, THOUGHT STEVE, IT WAS TIME TO MAKE A RADICAL LEAP FORWARD CAREER-WISE.

THANK YOU VERY MUCH.

I COULD PIMP...

I HAVE **GOT** TO FIND ANOTHER WAY TO MAKE A BUCK OTHER THAN GETTING MURDERERS AND CHILD ABUSERS OFF THE HOOK...

SAY! WHY DON'T YOU GET INTO CARTOONING? YEAH! THAT'S THE TICKET!

YEEOW!!

JAB!!

OO!

I HAVE **SOME** SCRUPLES, DUDE!

ANOTHER CAREER... I NEED ANOTHER CAREER... SOMETHING BIG MONEY... NO NECKTIES... LOOSE SEX...

OO!

..BUT **WHAT**? WHAT? WHAT? WHAT--

OO!

KNOCK! KNOCK!

BLECH

ACKTH COOP...

THAT'S IT! I'LL MANAGE A HEAVY-METAL GROUP!!

SMACK!

THPTT.

WELCOME TO OUR BASEMENT RECORDING STUDIO, FELLOW "DEATHTÖNGUE" MEMBERS. TODAY WE MAKE SOME DOUGH.

AS YOU KNOW, I'VE WRITTEN THE WORST HARD-CORE, METAL-CRUNCH MUSIC KNOWN IN THE FREE WORLD... AND WE'LL -- AH... A QUESTION FROM BILL?

WHISPER WHISPER WHISPER

ATTENTION! THERE WILL BE NO, REPEAT NO, DUETS WITH JULIO IGLESIAS THIS SESSION...

THPPT!

AWRIGHT...ONCE MORE FROM THE TOP...

EXCUSE ME, MR. PRODUCER.

ME AND THE BOYS WERE WONDERING HOW WE SHOULD APPROACH THE SECOND VERSE OF "DEMON DROOLER OF THE SEWER."

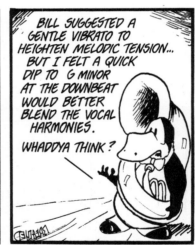

BILL SUGGESTED A GENTLE VIBRATO TO HEIGHTEN MELODIC TENSION... BUT I FELT A QUICK DIP TO G MINOR AT THE DOWNBEAT WOULD BETTER BLEND THE VOCAL HARMONIES.

WHADDYA THINK?

JUST WING THAT MOTHER.

JUST WING THAT MOTHER!

UH...MAY I SEE OUR DRUMMER AND TUBA PLAYER UP HERE... NOW.

I DON'T S'POSE EITHER OF YOU WOULD KNOW WHO'S BEEN MESSING WITH THE WORDS IN "LEPER LOVER"...

NOPE.   NOPE

"LEPER LOVER, CREATURE OF THE DARK. DRIP YOUR DISEASE, LEAVE YOUR MARK. THROUGH THE GUTTER SLIME AND STINKY...

"...GEORGE BUSH IS A TWINKIE."

HE DID IT.   DARN MY SOCIAL CONSCIENCE!

76

MEET DeathTöngue

"WILD" BILL CATT
—SINGER / LEAD TONGUE—

HOLD TIGHT, HEADBANGERS ...HERE COMES THE LOWEST, LOUDEST, LEWDEST BAD BOY OF METAL! AS THE TONGUE-STRUMMING, FRANTIC FÜHRER OF "DEATHTONGUE," HEAR HIM RAISE THE WIGS ON THEIR NEW ALBUM, "PIMPLES FROM HELL."

HODGE-PODGE
—DRUMS—

MASTER SKINS-BASHER HODGE LIVES FOR ONLY FOUR THINGS..."CHICKS, CHICKS, CHICKS" AND "DOUGH." BUT WHEN IT COMES TO DRUGS, THIS ROCK'N'ROLL PARTY ANIMAL "JUST SAYS NO."

OPUS CROAKUS
—RHYTHM TUBA—

THE SHORT AND SEXY BOSS TUBA ROCKER OF "DEATHTONGUE" WANTS ALL HIS FANS TO KNOW THAT DESPITE THE LIPSTICK, HAIR, EYE MAKEUP AND PANTY HOSE, HE ISN'T A SISSY.

SECRET "DEVIL" SIGN

STEVE DALLAS
SONGWRITER / MANAGER

AS THE "BRAINS BEHIND THE SPANDEX," STEVE HAS PENNED SUCH PAST HITS AS "SKATEBOARDING TO SATAN," "GUILLOTINE YOUR PARENTS," "CLEARASIL MESSIAH" AND THE CLASSIC TEEN ANTHEM "LET'S ROLL OVER LIONEL RICHIE WITH A TANK."

ROSEBUD WAS HAVING ONE OF THOSE DAYS. IN AN UNEXPLAINED FIT OF OPTIMISM, HE TRIED A LEAP OVER THE FENCE ON HOOPER'S RIDGE. MILO FOUND HIM SOME HOURS LATER.

I'M HAVING ONE OF THOSE DAYS.

WHAT HAPPENED?

WORD SPREAD QUICKLY AND A CRISIS-MANAGEMENT TEAM WAS DISPATCHED..

WE NEED A CRANE.

LET'S BLAST 'IM OFFA THERE!!

LET'S NOT PANIC, GENTLEMEN..

CRISIS CONTROL

THINGS WERE TRIED...

PULL! OUCH! PULLING!

AND OTHER THINGS WERE TRIED..

PUSH! OOF! PUSHING!

ARGH..

BUT IN THE HARSH FACE OF FUTILITY, ALL THERE WAS LEFT TO DO WAS FIND THE LARGER MEANING IN THIS DEBACLE...

MEN... I SEE THIS WHOLE THING AS A METAPHOR FOR THE LIMITS OF U.S. POWER.

OF COURSE!

GREAT. LET'S GO HOME AND HAVE A "POP TART."

AND SO.. AS THE LIVING SYMBOL OF AMERICA'S TROUBLED FOREIGN POLICY PRAYED FOR A LARGE SNOW DRIFT TO COME ALONG AND PROVIDE A DIGNIFIED ESCAPE, HE, TOO, REALIZED THAT BASSELOPES, LIKE NATIONS, SHOULD NEVER LET THEIR REACH EXCEED THEIR GRASP.

THE MORAL: I WANT A "POP TART."

LOLA! IF YOU DON'T AGREE TO END OUR SPAT, I SHALL BE FORCED TO BE VERY FORCEFUL AND PUT YOU OVER MY KNEE AND... ER.. AND... WELL, I'LL DO SOMETHING FORCEFUL!

MRS. GRANOLA!

I DROPPED BY FOR A SHORT VISIT.

WELL! I GUESS YOU'RE WONDERING ABOUT THESE --

I BROUGHT REV. WILDMON TO MEET BOTH OF YOU.

AH... DISASTER... DEBACLE... NAY, SOCIAL CATASTROPHE OF BIBLICAL PROPORTIONS...

OH, REVEREND! MY FUTURE DEMON-IN-LAW IS HERE!

WELL, NOW! MRS. GRANOLA ASKED IF I WOULD SIT DOWN WITH YOU KIDS BEFORE THE BIG DAY AND JUST... CHAT.

NOW, OPUS... DEEP DOWN, HOW DO YOU FEEL ABOUT MARRYING THIS LOVELY GIRL?

WHY, PRETTY GOOD! DARNED GOOD!

AND LOLA, HOW DO YOU FEEL ABOUT MARRYING A SHORT, WADDLING NIGHTMARE OF A GENE POOL.?

WELL...

I'M OUTTA HERE...

OPUS, MRS. GRANOLA SAYS YOU'RE A MUSICIAN... IS THAT ONE OF YOUR LITTLE SONGS THERE?

UH... IT'S JUST THE CHORUS... A SHORT REFRAIN, ACTUALLY...

MAY I?

"LET'S GUILLOTINE GRANDPA, .. GUILLOTINE GRANDPA, .. GUILLOTINE GRANDPA, AND PUT GRANDMA IN THE SOUP."

NOW, SEE.. IF HEARD IN CONTEXT...

LEONA! SOMETHING TO SLIP INTO THE HYMNS NEXT SUNDAY!

WELL, TIME TO GET BACK TO THE OL' PARISH. IT WAS NICE VISITING WITH YOU, SON.

LIKEWISE.

DON'T TELL MRS. GRANOLA, BUT I ENJOYED READING YOUR ROUSING LITTLE SONGS.

THANKS!

A SMALL BIT OF WISDOM BEFORE I LEAVE, DEAR BOY...

YES?

"CLEARASIL MESSIAH FROM THE SHELF" DOESN'T REALLY RHYME WITH "ZAPPING ZITS FROM HERE TO HELL."

RIGHT!

WHY DOESN'T YOUR MOTHER LIKE ME?

I DON'T KNOW. BUT REV. WILDMON DOES LIKE YOU. HE'S OUTSIDE TELLING HER RIGHT NOW.

SHE THINKS I MAKE TOO LITTLE MONEY.

NO, SHE DOESN'T.

I BELONG TO THE WRONG COUNTRY CLUB.

NO.

HE SITS IN THE FREEZER AND EATS FISH ENTRAILS...

NOW, LEONA...

WHERE'S STEVE, HODGE-PODGE?

IN LOS ANGELES WITH BILL, TRYING TO INTEREST A RECORD COMPANY.

INTEREST THEM IN **WHAT**?

THE MUSIC OF "DEATHTÖNGUE."

BUT THAT MUSIC GIVES PEOPLE INTESTINAL CRAMPS.

DON'T WORRY.. THEY'VE GOT AN ACE IN THE HOLE...

WELL, MR. CATT, WHEN STEVE HERE TELLS ME THAT YOU'RE PRONE TO BITING THE HEAD OFF A LIVE ROADIE ON STAGE, I SAY TO MYSELF, "CLIVE, THIS IS **DAMNED** EXCITING!"

CBS RECORDS

NOW, BESIDES BITING THE HEADS OFF ROADIES —-WHICH I LIKE!— WHAT ELSE IS YOUR ACT? ..THE VISUAL HOOK... GO ON... GIMME A SAMPLE...

♪ BWONG BWONG BWANG..

SAY! THIS IS GOOD! OH, THE KIDS WILL EAT THIS UP! WE'RE GONNA SELL RECORDS!

SNAP! SNAP!

BLEACK! BLEAHCK!

YEAH! BLEAHCK! RIGHT!

BBBTHPT! BBTHBPT!!

PLATINUM! CERTIFIED! I GOT GOOSE BUMPS!!

I LIKE THE LOOK OF "DEATHTÖNGUE".... "MTV" MAGIC! BUT WHAT ABOUT THE MUSIC, STEVE BABY?

LEMME RECITE FROM OUR HOTTEST NUMBER... DIG THIS...

♪ "MIDDLE-OF-THE-ROAD, MAN, IT STANKS LET'S RUN OVER LIONEL RICHIE WITH A TANK.."

WHADDYA THINK?

To Clive, Thanks! Lionel

YOU CAN SLAM THE DOOR BEHIND YOU.

THPPT.

SO YOU DIDN'T GET A RECORD CONTRACT?

NO. WE'RE COMING HOME TOMORROW.

WHAT'S ALL THAT NOISE?

WE'RE BACKSTAGE AT AN OZZY OSBOURNE CONCERT ...

BILL INSISTED ON MEETING THE "ELVIS" OF HEAVY METAL ...

THE LITTLE NIPS BLOODY WELL THREW ANOTHER BOTTLE AT ME!!

SIGH!

OZZY

81

I WAS BORN TOO LATE, ELEANOR. THINGS ARE MOVING TOO FAST. THE PERVERTS ARE RUNNING AMOK.

LAST NIGHT JOHNNY CARSON CAME OUT DRESSED AS SANTA CLAUS, WITH VANNA WHITE BARELY DRESSED AS HIS ELF. ELEANOR, THE WOMAN WAS FALLING OUT ALL OVER THE PLACE! I WAS REPULSED!

THIS COUNTRY IS GOING TO HELL IN A HANDBASKET IF IT DOESN'T RETURN TO SOME SENSIBLE VALUES.

SIDNEY! LISTEN! CHRISTMAS CAROLERS! OH, LET'S GO GREET THEM!

GREETINGS, JOYFUL MINSTRELS! WHAT SONG DO YOU HAVE FOR US TONIGHT?

"RUDOLPH THE RED-NOSED HEAD-BANGER" OR "I SAW MOMMY KISSING SANTA CLAUS SO I BLEW HIM AWAY." YOUR CHOICE!

THBLAT   BWONG!

WHO YA CALLING?   MY MOTHER.

EVERY CHRISTMAS I CALL KING GEORGE ISLAND IN ANTARCTICA LOOKING FOR MY REAL MOTHER... AND NOBODY EVER ANSWERS... SHE SENT ME NORTH FOR ADOPTION YEARS AGO... BUT I DON'T SEE WHY SHE WOULDN'T WANT TO TALK TO ME..

RIING! RIING!

I'M HER SON!! SHE CAN'T HIDE FROM THAT! THOSE ARE MY ROOTS DOWN THERE ON THE ROCKS AND ICE! WHY WON'T THEY ANSWER?! WHY, MILO?

RIING! RIING!

I DON'T KNOW. BUT I'M SURE SHE LOVES YOU.   WHY DOESN'T ANYBODY ANSWER?

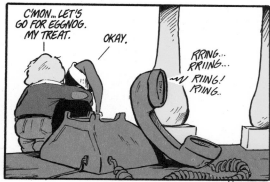

C'MON... LET'S GO FOR EGGNOG. MY TREAT.   OKAY.

RRING... RRIING... RIING! RIING..

RIING! RIING!   RIING!

NOBODY HAS A *@#!!# FOOTSTOOL?

CAN'T THIS WAIT TILL AFTER BREAKFAST?

GO ON!

POINT RESOLVE

I, STEVE DALLAS, RESOLVE FOR 1987 TO SMOKE, DRINK AND CAROUSE WITH TARTS AS MUCH AS HUMANLY POSSIBLE.

OUCH! AWRIGHT!

JAB!

...BUT NOT TO PUT ANTS INTO THE BEDS OF CLOSE ACQUAINTANCES NEXT NEW YEAR'S EVE.

LOUDER!

TRUDGE TRUDGE TRUDGE

POINT RESOLVE

SNAP!

POINT RESOLVE

I HAD A WEAK YEAR.

POINT RESOLVE

WHAT IS HAPPENING? OCCURRING? TRANSPIRING? GOING DOWN?

THE PRESIDENT IS STILL IN A LOT OF HOT WATER.

THEY HAVEN'T SETTLED THIS DISAGREEABLE BUSINESS YET?

NO. HE'S STONE-WALLING.

HE IS LOOKING DIFFERENT.

THE STRAIN IS TAKING ITS TOLL.

BURN THE TAPES.!!

NO, NO...

WHAT'S UP?

I THINK I'M ONTO A HOT STORY. I'VE GOT THE NEW "DEATHTÖNGUE" SINGLE, "HELL'S BELLS"...

RUMOR HAS IT THAT YOU CAN HEAR TERRIBLE MESSAGES IF YOU PLAY IT BACKWARD. LET'S GIVE IT A LISTEN...

GOOOO TO CHURCH... SAAAY YOOUR PRAYERS...

I DON'T THINK I HAVE A STORY.

TITHE.!. TITHE!

MILO, WHERE'S STEVE? WE HAVE BAND PRACTICE.

HE WENT FOR SOME MEDICAL TESTS...X-RAYS... HE HASN'T HAD A CHECK-UP FOR 17 YEARS.

MY GOODNESS!

WELL! I'M SURE YOU ALL JOIN US IN OUR HOPES THAT STEVE'S TESTS TURN OUT "A-OK"!...

CHECK AGAIN, MR. DALLAS... YOU'RE **SURE** YOU'RE BREATHING?

YES.

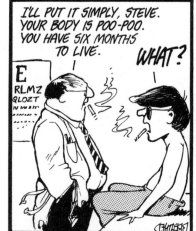

I'LL PUT IT SIMPLY, STEVE. YOUR BODY IS POO-POO. YOU HAVE SIX MONTHS TO LIVE.

WHAT?

..UNLESS YOU STOP SMOKING.

STOP SMOKING? YOU MEAN... ACTUALLY... SO TO SPEAK... STOP SMOKING?

COLD TURKEY. ZIP.

STOP SMOKING? NO CIGARETTES? WHAT YOU'RE TELLING ME, THEN, IS... JUST STOP SMOKING? JUST LIKE THAT?

...OR CROAK.

YA KNOW, DOC, A GUY COULD PACK A LOT OF LIVING INTO SIX MONTHS.

SO THAT'S IT. I QUIT SMOKING... OR I KICK OFF IN SIX MONTHS.

YA MEAN CIGARETTES... ARE UNHEALTHY?

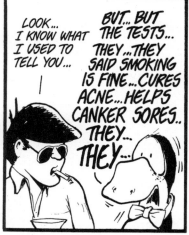

LOOK... I KNOW WHAT I USED TO TELL YOU...

BUT... BUT THE TESTS... THEY... THEY SAID SMOKING IS FINE... CURES ACNE... HELPS CANKER SORES.. THEY... THEY...

OPUS..!!

WHAT?

OL' BUDDY... THERE'S A CHANCE THE AMERICAN TOBACCO INSTITUTE'S HEALTH RESEARCH IS... WELL... BIASED.

GOOD LORD.

WHAT'S WITH BLOB-BUTT?

"IRANGATE" HAS OPUS A LITTLE SHAKEN...

AND THEN STEVE'S SMOKING-RELATED HEALTH PROBLEMS BLUNTLY EXPOSED THE HOMICIDAL HYPOCRISY OF AN ENTIRE INDUSTRY.

I THINK HE'S TRYING TO REACH A CONCLUSION REGARDING THE FAITH WE ALL LIKE TO HAVE IN OUR CORPORATE AND POLITICAL INSTITUTIONS...

NO, VIRGINIA, THERE REALLY ISN'T A SANTA CLAUS...

FELLOW "DEATHTÖNGUERS," I'D LIKE TO ANNOUNCE THAT I'LL BE TRYING TO QUIT SMOKING THIS WEEK.

IN FACT, I JUST NOW GAVE AWAY NEARLY EVERY SINGLE "MARLBORO" I OWN.

COUGH. GAG...

FRANKLY, I THINK THAT DESERVES SOME CONGRATULATIONS, DON'T YOU? HELLO?

CONGRAT-ULATIONS.

THANKS.

BILL'S BAZOOKA-BARFING.

WHAT IN THE WORLD ARE YOU DOING, SIR?

HAZARDOUS DUTY. I'M GOING TO ASSIST MY GOOD FRIEND STEVE IN KICKING CIGARETTES COLD TURKEY.

AH. THANK YOU ALL FOR COMING OUT TO SEE ME OFF ON MY MISSION. WITH YOUR PRAYERS, I SHALL RETURN SAFELY.

HE'S SO BRAVE! =THPPT!=

THIS IS SO EMOTIONAL...

IF ANYTHING SHOULD...UH, HAPPEN... I'LL SEE TO—

I KNOW. THANK YOU.

GOD... IS MY COPILOT.

GET IN HERE AND TIE ME UP, YOU IDIOT.

MAKE IT TIGHT. AND WHATEVER I SAY, DON'T RELEASE ME. HOW MANY MINUTES SINCE MY LAST SMOKE?

I STILL FEEL IN CONTROL. MIND OVER MATTER... I THINK I'M GONNA ACE THIS!

37.

GET ME A ★@!!# CIGARETTE BEFORE I STICK YOU IN A BLENDER.

38.

OPUS... ALL FUN ASIDE... UNTIE ME AND SHOW ME WHERE YOU HID MY SMOKES... OPUS?... I'M SERIOUS...

OPUS?

I NEED A SMOKE, OPUS... MY...MY HEAD FEELS FUNNY...MY

...MY FEET ARE TURNING INTO PUDDLES!

AARRGH...

INTO THE ABYSS!

OOF!

CLUMP!

CLUMP!

STEVE...NO! I PROMISED I WOULDN'T LET YOU HAVE ANY OF THESE... STEVE... **STEVE!**

NOW LOOK! JUST STOP AND GET A GRIP ON YOURSELF... AND CONSIDER CALMLY AND RATIONALLY THE SIMPLE VIRTUES OF SELF-RESTRAINT...

AARRGGH- OOF! ARGH! CLUMP! CLUMP!

JUST IMAGINE... NORMALLY I'D BE HAVING A ROOT BEER AND WATCHING "GENERAL HOSPITAL" RIGHT NOW..

THWUNK!

MILO, WHY ARE YOU PEERING AT THE BOARDINGHOUSE FROM UP HERE?

STEVE AND OPUS ARE INSIDE...

AND STEVE IS GOING COLD TURKEY FROM CIGARETTES.

BUT... EVEN WITH NICOTINE **IN** HIS BLOODSTREAM, STEVE IS A MANIAC!

WELL, LOLA, THAT'S WHY WE'RE UP **HERE.**

WHERE'D YA HIDE 'EM?!...

HELLO? POLICE?

POUND! POUND! POUND!

VIRGIL, THERE'S A PENGUIN ON THE PHONE. SEZ HE'S CALLING FROM INSIDE A TOILET BOWL...

..SEZ THERE'S A MADMAN IN HIS UNDERWEAR JUMPING UP AND DOWN ON THE LID, THREATENING HIS LIFE.

IS IT URGENT?

IS IT URGENT?

SEZ THE "TY-D-BOWL" IS IRRITATING HIS BUTTOCKS.

HANG UP.

WHAT'S HAPPENING DOWN THERE, MILO?

DON'T GET TOO CLOSE!

WAIT! STEVE'S AT THE WINDOW!...

HE'S FROTHING AT THE MOUTH! ...HE'S GOT OPUS BY THE NECK! I THINK HE'S SAYING SOMETHING...

CAN YOU MAKE IT OUT?

"A...A CARTON OF CAMELS BY NOON OR PERMANENT PENGUIN PÂTÉ."

OPUS! QUICK! ESCAPE THIS WAY! BEFORE HE SEES US!...

=SIGH=

IT'S ALL OVER, MILO. STEVE IS INSIDE... SAFELY NEUTRALIZED.

A SUITABLE ANTIDOTE FOR NICOTINE WITHDRAWAL WAS DISCOVERED... THANK GOODNESS!

BLOATED AND GORGED, THE FORMER TOBACCO ADDICT WAS REMOVED WITH DIFFICULTY FROM THE NOW-EMPTY PANTRY...

FEARS OF A SPONTANEOUS EXPLOSION SPREAD AND A BOMB SQUAD WAS CALLED. STEVE WAS PUT TO BED WITHOUT INCIDENT AND SLEPT FOR THREE DAYS.

THE NICOTINE-WITHDRAWAL PROCESS WAS CALLED A SUCCESS. STEVE'S STRENGTH OF CHARACTER WAS CITED.

HOWEVER, IN JULY, STEVE ENTERED THE BETTY FORD CLINIC FOR TREATMENT OF ADDICTION TO "DING DONGS." THE PATIENT WAS FORCIBLY DISCHARGED SOME WEEKS LATER.

SOME OF US WERE WONDERING HOW YOUR ROMANCE WITH LOLA GRANOLA IS COMING ALONG.

WE WERE WATCHING A SYLVESTER STALLONE MOVIE LAST NIGHT AND SHE WAS SALIVATING.

YE OLDE PONDER PATCH

I ASKED HER IF **MY** BODY TURNED HER ON... AND DO YOU KNOW WHAT SHE SAID?

WHAT?

SHE SAID ALL SHE WANTS OUT OF A LOVER PHYSICALLY ARE "LIPS TO KISS AND A SHOULDER TO CRY ON."

THAT'S VERY SWEET.

I'M SHORT ON BOTH COUNTS.!!

YE OLDE PONDER PATCH

ARNOLD SCHWARTZENEGGER... MY GOD...THE MAN'S BODY IS... INHUMAN.

DON'T FOR A MINUTE THINK THAT I DON'T LOVE YOU EXACTLY THE WAY YOU ARE, HANDSOME.

IF I MAY MAKE AN ASIDE HERE, NOTE THAT MY "SIGNIFICANT OTHER" IS ON THE BRINK OF ENTERING THE CONVERSATIONAL ZONE OF A RELATIONSHIP THAT MANY OF US KNOW AS "THE BIG LIE." LISTEN.

PERSONALLY, I THINK THAT REALLY....**HUGE** MUSCLES ARE GROSS.

RIGHT.

"THE SCHWARTZENEGGER CHEST EXPANDER"... - INCREASE CHEST SIZE AND SEX APPEAL EXPONENTIALLY."

AARGH..

AAAIGH!!

BLOOM BOARDING HOUSE NO VACANCY

Local resident found unconscious with chest hair mysteriously ripped out

Police and medical experts are still trying to piece together the events surrounding yesterday's discovery of a small man who recently had all his chest hair violently torn out. He had apparently passed out from pain.

"Recovering nicely"

"did it hurt?" said the victim...

94

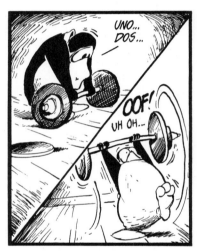

97

THERE'LL BE NO COMIC TODAY, LADIES AND GENTLEMEN. "BLOOM COUNTY PRODUCTIONS" IS UNDER SUSPENSION.

THE N.A.C.P.* CONDUCTED SURPRISE DRUG TESTS ON OUR PLAYERS THIS MORNING... AND SOME NUT CAME UP POSITIVE...

* "NATIONAL ASSOCIATION OF COMIC PRODUCERS"

THE ENTIRELY UNCALLED—FOR DISCIPLINARY ACTION INCLUDES THE CANCELLATION OF TODAY'S PROFIT—-ER, PERFORMANCE.

IN THE MEANTIME, ALL CAST MEMBERS ARE CONFINED TO THE DRESSING ROOM UNTIL WE FIND OUT EXACTLY **WHO'S BEEN TAKING WHAT AROUND HERE.!!**

SLAM!

WAS IT YOU?

NO, IT WAS **NOT** ME.

WHOEVER IT WAS, WHAT'D THEY TAKE?

ANABOLIC STEROIDS, I HEAR.

EXCUSE ME... I WONDER IF––

VALENTINE'S DAY SINGLES MINGLES 5:00

HERE. TAKE THIS BEFORE WE GO ANY FURTHER.

WHAT IS IT?

MY SEXUAL HISTORY. NAMES, NUMBERS AND ADDRESSES ARE ALL UP TO DATE.

THANK YOU.

...AND IF YOU'LL PLEASE FILL OUT THESE FORMS DETAILING ALL YOUR PAST INTIMATE PHYSICAL CONTACTS WITHIN THE LAST FIVE YEARS...

I HAVEN'T HAD ANY.

NONE?

NONE WHATSOEVER?

NOPE. I'M QUITE THE PRUDE.

I'M INTO PRUDES!

ME TOO!

I SAW HIM FIRST!!

BOY! ALL THIS PAPERWORK, JUST FOR DIRECTIONS TO THE MEN'S ROOM!

THE HORN SECTION FOR "DEATHTÖNGUE" APPEARS IDLE. WHAT'S UP?

STEVE AND BILL HAVE BEEN SUMMONED TO WASHINGTON.

THEY WERE SUBPOENAED?

YES. AND WE ALL KNOW HOW PAINFUL A PROCEDURE THAT CAN BE FOR A MALE OVER 30.

THEY MUST BE TESTIFYING AT THE SPECIAL SENATE HEARINGS ON "PORN ROCK."

..AND PUTTING FORTH A GOOD FIGHT, ONE MIGHT HOPE.

"COOPERATION," MADAM COMMITTEE CHAIRWOMAN, IS OUR SECOND NAME...

SOLD MY SOUL TO ROCK 'N' ROLL! ACK!

MR. DALLAS, I BELIEVE THIS IS ONE OF YOUR "DEATHTÖNGUE" SONGS. LET'S REVIEW IT TOGETHER.

"LEMME GRAZE INTO YOUR VELDT, LEMME STOMPLE YOUR ALBINO, LEMME NIBBLE ON YOUR BUDS, I'M YOUR... UH..."

..LOVE RHINO.

"LOVE RHINO."

OFF WITH HIS HEAD.

♪ TWANG! TWANG!

TAP TAP TAP

WELL, MR. DALLAS... WE'VE HEARD YOUR SMUT MASQUERADING AS SONGS...

...AND WE'VE HEARD HOW TEEN PROSTITUTION, PREGNANCY, DRUG USE, CULTS, RUNAWAYS, SUICIDE AND POOR HYGIENE ARE SWEEPING THIS NATION.

WE THOUGHT YOU MIGHT LIKE TO SHARE WITH THE COMMITTEE ANY PARTICULAR CAUSES YOU MIGHT SEE FOR THOSE LATTER PROBLEMS...

I DUNNO. MAYBE THE PROLIFERATION OF NARROW, SUFFOCATING ZEALOTRY MASQUERADING AS PARENTING IN THIS COUNTRY.

OFF WITH HIS HEAD.

WE CAN'T DO THAT, TIPPY!

AWRIGHT... **AWRIGHT**... I'LL CONCEDE THAT THE NAME "DEATHTÖNGUE" IS NOT PARTICULARLY CONDUCIVE TO POSITIVE, CHRISTIAN, ALL-AMERICAN THOUGHT IN OUR NATION'S YOUTH...

WHICH...UH..WHICH, OF COURSE, IS WHY WE CHANGED OUR NAME LAST WEEK TO...ER...TO...

..."BILLY AND THE BOINGERS."

"BOINGERS"? WHAT'S A "BOINGER"?

SOUNDS VAGUELY WHOLESOME.

STEVE'S CAVING IN !!

MILO !! DID YOU JUST SEE THE HORROR THEY SHOWED ON TV ?!

WHAT? WHAT?

STEVE JUST BUCKLED UNDER SENATE PRESSURE AND CHANGED "DEATHTÖNGUE'S" NAME TO 'BILLY AND THE BOINGERS"! ON TV !!

OH. I THOUGHT THEY WERE SHOWING CROSS SECTIONS OF THE PRESIDENT'S BLADDER AGAIN.

NO, NO, NO...

...OR MORE GRAPHIC DIAGRAMS OF THE PRESIDENT'S PROSTATE.

FORGET IT.

YA KNOW, FOR MY MONEY, YOU NEVER CAN SEE TOO MUCH OF THAT SORT OF THING.

NOBODY GIVE ME ANY TROUBLE.

"BILLY AND THE BOINGERS"?

IT WAS ALL I COULD THINK OF...

SOMEHOW, IT JUST DOESN'T CHALLENGE THE SENSIBILITIES OF THE TRADITIONAL ESTABLISHMENT.

SORRY. IT'S OFFICIAL NOW.

SAY... MAYBE "BOINGER" HAS SOME UGLY, UNSAVORY CONNOTATION WE HAVEN'T THOUGHT OF !

AWAY, KNAVES !

MIGHT IT BE A VAGUE SEXUAL EUPHEMISM ?

NO, THAT'D BE "BILLY AND THE DIDDLERS."

100

LOLA... DO YOU THINK YOU COULD STAND BEING MARRIED TO A... "BOINGER"?

SURE.

I SUPPOSE IT BEATS BEING MARRIED TO A "DEATHTÖNGUER."

YES, BUT IT DOESN'T BEAT BEING MARRIED TO KEITH RICHARDS.

YOU KNOW, I HYPERVENTILATE WHEN YOU SAY THINGS LIKE THAT.

I'M SORRY.

AN AIR OF... DANGEROUS EXPECTATION HANGS HEAVY IN THE OFFICES OF THE MIGHTY BLOOM PICAYUNE...

IT WAS FINALLY TIME FOR A TRULY FRANK ARTICLE ON THE PUBLIC-HEALTH THREAT OF AIDS... AND CHIEF EDITOR ARMAND DIPTHONG KNEW THAT WHAT HIS READERS NEEDED WAS... BRUTALLY EXPLICIT SEXUAL ADVICE...

EASY...

COURAGE, BOSS... SLOW 'N' EASY... YOU CAN DO IT...

"DON'T FOOL AROUND!!"

TRY IT AGAIN, BOSS!

TAP TAP TAP

COPY BOY! COPY BOY!

HERE'S THE "AIDS AND PUBLIC HEALTH" STORY. I... I TRIED TO BE AS EXPLICIT AS POSSIBLE...

"IT'S WISE TO AVOID (THE 'I' WORD) OR (THE 'A' WORD) WITH (THE 'H' WORD) IN EITHER HIS OR HER (THE 'A' WORD II) AFTER (THE 'L' WORD) WITHOUT A BRAND-NAME ('C' WORD)."

AM I WAFFLING?

YOU'RE WAFFLING.

BOSS... I THINK TODAY'S **AIDS** STORY WAS TOO WISHY-WASHY, AS USUAL...

YOUR FREQUENT USE OF THE TERM "INTIMATE CONTACT" HAS LEFT SOME OF OUR READERS CONFUSED.

I TRIED.

MRS. DILLWHIPPLE IS ON THE PHONE.

AGAIN?

MRS. DILLWHIPPLE COULD WELL USE A LITTLE EXPLICITNESS IN HER LIFE.

YES, MADAM, YOU MAY CONTINUE TO SAFELY KISS YOUR CAT "WOOGUMS" FULL ON THE LIPS...

ATTENTION, EVERYBODY! I HAVE JUST SUCCEEDED IN WRITING A SHOCKINGLY BLUNT STORY ON SEX AND PUBLIC HEALTH.

BRACE YOURSELVES. WE MAY WELL LOSE ALL 14 SUBSCRIPTIONS OF THE "LADIES' CHURCH MUFFIN CLUB."

BUT NO MATTER! EVEN AS I SPEAK, COPY BOY MILO IS FETCHING VARIOUS OFFENSIVE AND EMBARRASSING WORDS FROM OUR **FORBIDDEN-WORD VAULT** TO MAKE THIS STORY A REALITY!!

GOT 'EM!!

THE STORY ON SEX AND PUBLIC HEALTH APPEARED IN THE NEXT MORNING'S PICAYUNE... EXPLICIT, YET INFORMATIVE.

AS EXPECTED, THE ENTIRE MEMBERSHIP OF THE "LADIES' CHURCH MUFFIN CLUB" CANCELED THEIR SUBSCRIPTIONS. THE REPUBLIC, IN GENERAL, REMAINED STRONG, HOWEVER.

YES, MOST JUST TOOK THE OFFENSIVE WORDS AND EMBARRASSING ANATOMICAL REFERENCES FULLY IN STRIDE...

..OTHERS, OF A MORE SENSITIVE CONSTITUTION... DID NOT.

OH OH OH OH

103

BINKLEY?... WHAT'S ALL THAT NOISE IN THERE?

IT'S MY ANXIETY CLOSET, DAD... THEY'RE GOING TO BRING OUT ME AS I'LL BE TWENTY YEARS FROM NOW.

WHY, HOW VERY PROVOCATIVE!

I'M TERRIBLY ANXIOUS. I DON'T KNOW WHAT I'LL ASK HIM.

YOU'LL THINK OF SOMETHING, SON.

WHAT WOULD YOU ASK A 30-YEAR-OLD ME?

I'D ASK HIM IF YOU'RE STILL LOOPY AS A LOON.

AS I STAND BEFORE MY PRIVATE PORTAL OF PARANOIA, I AWAIT THE MEETING OF MYSELF... AS I WILL BE TWENTY YEARS FROM NOW...

THE PHILOSOPHICAL IMPLICATIONS BOGGLE THE NOODLE! WHAT DOES A FELLOW ASK HIS OLDER SELF??

WHEN—?

AROUND ABOUT PUBERTY.

WELL, OLDER SELF... I GUESS I HAVE TO ASK THE BIG QUESTIONS...

THAT'S WHY I'M HERE.

DID I...ER, WE MANAGE TO GET THROUGH FIFTH GRADE WITHOUT STRANGLING LIZZIE "THE LIZARD" BLACKHEAD?

YES.

DID WE... FINISH COLLEGE?

BARELY.

DID WE... ≶GULP≶ GET MARRIED?

REMEMBER "LIZARD" BLACKHEAD?

WE MARRIED LIZZIE "THE LIZARD" BLACKHEAD?!

WE CALL HER "QUEEN ELIZABETH" NOW. COME... FOLLOW ME INTO YOUR FUTURE WORLD, YOUNGER SELF...

THIS UGLY LITTLE DWELLING IS OUR HOUSE. WE CALL IT "BINKLEY MANOR." WE MOVED HERE IN 1998. THAT'S OUR '93 VOLKSWAGEN. WE CALL IT OUR "LITTLE LAMBORGHINI."

IT'S ALL A WAY OF SOMEHOW DEALING WITH THE MEDIOCRITY OF OUR ADULT LIFE... AND THE FAILED DREAMS OF OUR YOUTH. **YOUR** YOUTH.

HEY... THERE'S A GOPHER WETTING ON MY FOOT...

BAD DOG, RAMBO... BAD DOG!

THIS IS WHERE WE WORK? WHAT IS IT?

THE FEDERAL SELF-TYING SHOELACE PLANT.

REALLY? DID WE INVENT IT?

NO, WE JUST SWEEP UP.

OH.

BUT WE DID PERSONALLY LEAD AN ILLEGAL UNION STRIKE AGAINST THE GOVERNMENT AND CLOSED THE PLANT DOWN IN THE FALL OF 2005...

REALLY?!

..BUT THEN PRESIDENT SPRINGSTEEN FIRED EVERYBODY.

SO THIS IS IT? A MOUSY WIFE NAMED "QUEEN ELIZABETH" AND AN UGLY DOG NAMED "RAMBO"?

I'M AFRAID SO...

..WE FEARED THE RISKS NEEDED TO EXCEL IN LIFE... AND NOW LIVE A COWARDLY FACADE TO MASK OUR DISAPPOINTED HOPES.

COME... MEET YOUR FUTURE DAUGHTER.

DAUGHTER?!

OH, DOLLY? ...DOLLY PARTON BINKLEY!

DOLLY... SAY HELLO TO THE YOUNGER ME.

OH, NO. OOOOo.

HELLO, WORMBUTT.

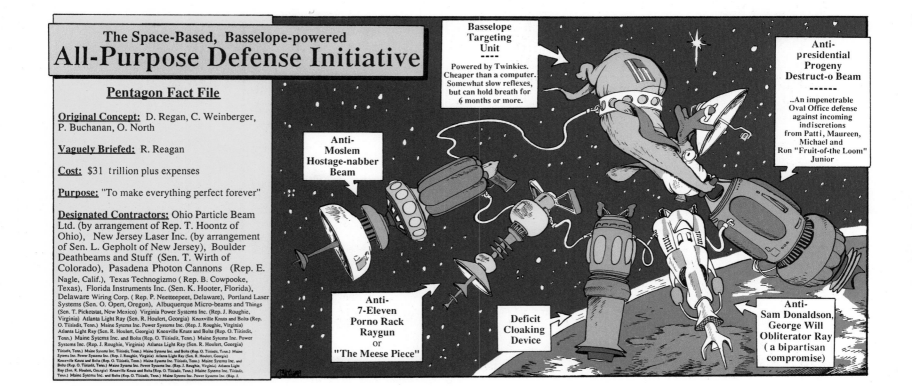

IT'S A TRUISM, YA KNOW.

WHAT'S A TRUISM?

THAT GREAT-LOOKING GALS ALWAYS SEEM TO BE WITH GOOFY-LOOKING GUYS.

THAT'S NOT TRUE.

TAKE US. YOU'RE A KNOCKOUT. AND I LOOK LIKE THE PILLSBURY DOUGH-BOY AFTER GETTING TOO NEAR THE STOVE.

THAT'S NOT TRUE.

THIS... **THIS** IS AN EXAMPLE OF THE CHRISTIE BRINKLEY-BILLY JOEL SYNDROME!

ACTUALLY... UPON CLOSER EXAMINATION... MY FEATURES AREN'T BEYOND ALL HOPE...

HMM ....PULL IN THE SCHNOZZ A BIT...BRING OUT THE CHIN...LOWER THE BROW... AND WHAT WOULD WE HAVE?

DAVID LETTERMAN.

GREAT **SCOTT**. IT'S WORSE THAN I IMAGINED!

WHATCHYA READIN', OPUS?

AN INDEX TO DIET BOOKS. I FIGURE IF NOTHING ELSE, I CAN IMPROVE MY WEIGHT.

HOW ABOUT EATING LESS, AND EXERCISE.

HERE'S SOMETHING! "THE BROCCOLI-BROTH AND BEAN-BATH DIET"!

NAW. TOO WEIRD. I NEED SOMETHING BASIC.

HOW ABOUT EATING LESS, AND EXERCISE.

"DR. FRANK'S FROG LEGS, FIGS AND FLATULENCE DIET"! WHADDYA THINK?!

THE DIET GUERRILLA SURVEYS THE DAMAGE: TWO BROKEN RIBS... A CONCUSSION... ONE BADLY BRUISED BUTTOCK AREA...

JEEZ LAWEEZ...

THE REMAINING DIET ALTERNATIVE IS NOT PLEASANT TO CONSIDER... YET CONSIDER HE MUST...

NO NO NO NO NO NO

..EAT LESS AND EXERCISE!!

AAAIGH!!

HONEY, THERE JUST AIN'T ANOTHER WAY.

OH HUSH **UP**, OPRAH.

WELL, POP... WHAT DO **YOU** THINK?

WHAT DO I THINK ABOUT WHAT?

OLLIE NORTH... FAWN HALL...

FAWN HALL... OLLIE NORTH...

WHAT I THINK IS THAT THIS STRIP ALREADY HAS ENOUGH LIBEL PROBLEMS.

LADIES AND GENTLEMEN... OUR LAWYERS HAVE ORDERED US TO RETRACT THE "IMPLICATIONS" OF YESTERDAY'S PANEL... ALTHOUGH WE HONESTLY DON'T KNOW WHAT THEY'RE TALKING ABOUT.

IT FEATURED LT. COL. OLLIE NORTH...

... AND HIS SECRETARY, ANNETTE FUNICELLO.

WHATEVER IT WAS, WE RETRACT IT.

THE LAWYERS WANT A WORD WITH YOU OUT IN THEIR LIMO.

DEEP IN THE BOWELS OF THE BLOOM BOARDING HOUSE, A DARING EXPERIMENT IS BEING CONDUCTED... A BOLD AND FRIGHTENING FORAY INTO THE DARKEST FORBIDDEN RECESSES OF THE HUMAN UNIVERSE....

NOW LET'S SAY HELLO TO MY LOVELY CO-HOST... VANNA WHITE! OH, VANNA!!

CLAP! CLAP! CLAP!

HOOT!

OUR DEFENDING CHAMPION, WALLY ICKSTEIN, IS BACK AND READY TO WIN. SPIN THE WHEEL, WALLY.

OKAY, PAT.

IS THERE AN "E"?

RIGHT YOU ARE. ONE. CAN YOU GUESS THE PHRASE, WALLY?

I'LL TAKE A WILD STAB AT IT...

"TEA CUP"?

RIGHT!

STOP THE EXPERIMENT!!

VEGETABLE MATTER, GENTLEMEN... WE HAVE VEGETABLE MATTER!!

MY GOODNESS...

HE'S AN EGGPLANT!

THANK GOD WE WEREN'T PLAYING JOAN RIVERS, OR HE'D BE A SALAD.

Editor's Note:

DUE TO OVERWHELMING READER REQUESTS, WE PRESENT THE FOLLOWING "REQUEST" SPECIAL:

ALL ABOUT POLO

... AN INTRODUCTION TO THE EXCITING SPORT THAT COMBINES THE THRILL OF CROQUET WITH THE SKILLS OF ROY ROGERS ...

(A) SUITING UP: HERE WE SEE THE GREAT POLO PLAYER PULLING ON HIS OSTRICH-LEATHER "SPATOS." THE GIRAFFE-BONE MALLET BESIDE HIM IS CALLED A "WONKER." HIS COLOGNE IS CALVIN KLEIN'S "OBSESSION."

OOF

Bloom County Polo Club
NONMEMBERS WILL BE SHOT.

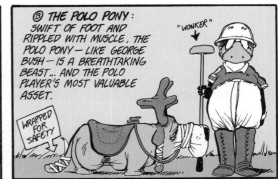

(B) THE POLO PONY: SWIFT OF FOOT AND RIPPLED WITH MUSCLE, THE POLO PONY — LIKE GEORGE BUSH — IS A BREATHTAKING BEAST... AND THE POLO PLAYER'S MOST VALUABLE ASSET.

"WONKER"

WRAPPED FOR SAFETY

(C) PLAYING THE GAME: WE HAVEN'T THE FOGGIEST AS TO WHAT THE OBJECT OF POLO IS, BUT IT SEEMS TO INVOLVE A GREAT DEAL OF GALLOPING ABOUT, SWINGING AT BALLS AND HORSE SWEAT.

HERE WE SEE DEMONSTRATED THE CLASSIC "PRINCE CHARLES TECHNIQUE"...

WHOOSH!!

ZING!

WHACK!!

(D) THE POST-MATCH WIND-DOWN WITH BLOODY MARYS AT THE CLUB POOL:

I SAID I WAS SORRY. HERE. READ A "VANITY FAIR."

I TINK WE TOULD LOOK FOR MY NODE AGAIN.

UPCOMING "REQUEST" SPECIAL: "ALL ABOUT MICHAEL J. FOX'S PITUITARY PROBLEMS."

THE WHOLE THING STARTED AROUND DINNERTIME IN THE BOARDINGHOUSE LAST TUESDAY...

DAD, I DON'T THINK WE SHOULD EAT MEAT ANYMORE.

I HAVE CONCLUDED THAT IT IS AN IMMORAL DISTINCTION TO SAY KILLING A COW IS ANY LESS WRONG THAN KILLING, SAY, A WHALE.

MUNCH MUNCH

YOU DO FIND THE DESTRUCTION OF SEA MAMMALS IMMORAL, DON'T YOU?

ANY GOOD AMERICAN DOES, SON.

GOOD! THIS IS NOW A MEAT-FREE ZONE! LONG LIVE THE VEGETABLE!

BY GOD, LET'S EAT A PEA FOR A PORPOISE!!

SO BESIDES BEEF, PORK, CHICKEN AND FISH, WE SHOULDN'T EAT DAIRY PRODUCTS EITHER, SON?

RIGHT.

TAKING A MORAL STAND IS AN EXERCISE IN PHILOSOPHICAL PURITY. ABUSING AND CONFINING ANIMALS FOR THEIR MILK AND EGGS IS NO MORE ACCEPTABLE THAN KILLING THEM.

I HEREBY DECLARE THIS HOUSE FREE OF ANY EXPLOITATION OF OUR WILD BRETHREN FOR THEIR FLESH!

WHERE THE HELL ARE ALL MY SHOES?

...OR THEIR SKIN!

FELLOW BOARDERS! I'M TALKING ABOUT THE SANCTITY OF ALL LIFE! CAN ANY OF YOU TURN TO ANOTHER AND SAY THAT HE OR SHE IS SUPERIOR BY VIRTUE OF SPECIES? OR BRAIN SIZE? OR WHETHER ONE HAS HAIR ON THE SOLES OF ONE'S FEET? WELL?!

BINKLEY HAD THEM THERE. THEY COULDN'T. HENCE, IT WAS VOTED THAT AS OF MIDNIGHT, THEY WOULD ALL BE NON-LEATHER-WEARING VEGETARIANS.

HAIR?

AN EXODUS OF ANIMAL PRODUCTS IMMEDIATELY BEGAN. THE DEADLINE APPROACHED AND COMPLIANCE LOOKED GOOD...

...HOWEVER, SOME HOARDING WAS REPORTED.

QUICK, MAN! 20 DOZEN McNUGGETS TO GO!! AND MAKE IT SNAPPY!!

McDonald's

WATCH WHERE YOU'RE STEPPING!!

IT MAY NOT BE CUTE AND FURRY, BUT THAT SNAIL HAS THE SAME RIGHT TO LIVE OUT ITS LIFE AS A BABY HARP SEAL DOES.

WE EAT THEM, WE WEAR THEM...WE TORTURE THEM FOR SCIENCE...WE POISON THEM ON OUR CROPS...AND WE EVEN **WALK** ON THEM!!

WE'VE GOT TO TAKE ACTION ON THIS!!

SNAIL, I DON'T MUCH LIKE WHERE THIS IS ALL DRIFTING.

THEIR MURDEROUS FEET SUSPENDED SAFELY ABOVE THEIR UNSEEN BRETHREN IN THE SPRING GRASS BELOW, THE NON-MEAT EATING, NON-PESTICIDE-TREATED-VEGETABLE EATING, NON-ANIMAL-TESTED-MEDICINE USING, NON-DAIRY CONSUMING, STRICTLY COTTON AND POLYESTER WEARING "CRITTER DEFENDERS" PONDER THE HAPPY FACT THAT THEY ARE FINALLY...TOTALLY...COMPLETELY COEXISTING IN PEACE WITH ALL LIFE ON THIS PLANET...

HOLD IT! WE'RE BREATHING AND MASSACRING MILLIONS OF GERMS!!

BINKLEY...EVERYBODY'S HUNGRY. COME ON DOWN. WE PROMISE TO KEEP THE EXPLOITATION OF ANY ANIMALS TO A MINIMUM.

NO! I WILL **NOT** ACCEPT THAT MORAL PURITY IS IMPOSSIBLE!!

BINKLEY, GOD SAYS THOU SHALT NOT KILL...BUT WE REGULARLY KILL IN GOD'S NAME. DESPITE WHAT THEY TELL YOU, THERE SIMPLY ARE NO MORAL ABSOLUTES IN A COMPLEX WORLD.

EXCEPT THAT I'M ABSOLUTELY STARVING FOR A PIZZA.

HECK, WE'LL HAVE 'EM HOLD THE ANCHOVIES.

GREAT. OUR WORLD TOUR IS A GIG AT AN ALBUQUERQUE "MOOSE LODGE" AND OUR CORPORATE SPONSOR SELLS "ODOR-EATERS."

WHAT FURTHER INDIGNITIES COULD POSSIBLY LIE AHEAD?

SAY, OPUS...

..YA KNOW THE TREND OF TV ACTORS LIKE BRUCE WILLIS AND DON JOHNSON PRETENDING THEY'RE ROCK STARS, HIRING MUSICIANS AND THEN CUTTING AN ALBUM?

YES. SO WHO'S ON THE PHONE?

DON KNOTTS.

AWRIGHT, LET'S GET THOSE AMPS LOADED IN THE WINNEBAGO...WE GOTTA MAKE NEW MEXICO BY SIX a.m...!

I THOUGHT I HIRED YOU AS ROADIE.

YA DID.

BOINGER'S WORLD TOUR 87

WELL?

I SUB-CONTRACTED OUT.

WHICH WAY TO ALBUQUER-QUE?

Dr. Scholl's ODOR-EATERS PRESENTS THE BOINGERS

SCREEECH!! CAREEEN!!

WUMP!!

BANG!! CRUNCH CHUNKA CHUNKA

TOUR 87

HE WAS SLEEPING!!

WAS NOT! MY EYELIDS WERE MEDITATING!

116

HALFWAY TO ALBUQUERQUE, THE GREAT BOINGERS WORLD TOUR BUS STOPPED FOR THE NIGHT...

TV DINNERS WERE WARMED WHILE THE STRESSES OF THE ROAD SLOWLY GAVE WAY TO THE SHARED COMFORT OF MALE COMRADERY.

EVENTUALLY, CONVERSATION TURNED TO THE SORT OF THINGS INTROSPECTIVE, SENSITIVE MEN TALK ABOUT OVER WARM ROOT BEERS AT 2:37 a.m....

I LIKE WOMEN WITH BIG, FULL... SHOULDER BLADES.

YEAH.

YEAH.

THPT.

UH.. GOOD MORNING, OFFICER...

HOWDY, BOY! SAY, THAT WOULDN'T BE ONE O' THEM FANCY RADAR DE-TECTORS, WOULD IT, BOY?

THIS? UH...WHY, NO...ACTUALLY, THIS IS A... ER... AN OFFICIAL "CAPTAIN KIRK SUB-SPACE COMMUNICATOR"... YEAH... THAT'S RIGHT!

UH... HELLO? STARFLEET COMMAND? COME IN, PLEASE... HELLO?

ROAD KING

FUZZ BUSTER

NO ANSWER.

MUSTA BROKE BACK THERE WHEN YEW WAS DOIN' WARP 70.

I WANTED TO GO OVER THE RULES WITH YOU GUYS BEFORE WE GOT TO THE BIG GIG AT THE MOOSE LODGE...

1987 BOINGERS WORLD TOUR

NO BOOZIN', NO SPITTIN', NO MOONING THE AUDIENCE... NO... UH...

HOLD IT.

WHO'S DRIVING?!

KEEP YER PANTS ON. I PUSHED CRUISE CONTROL.

118

THAT'S RIGHT. I'M THE TUBA PLAYER.

I'M PAUL YOUNGBLATT, ENTERTAINMENT DIRECTOR FOR TONIGHT'S BANQUET. I HAVE A REQUEST.

THE ENTIRE MOOSE WIVES' AUXILIARY HAVE ASKED IF YOU ALL WOULD PLAY A BARRY MANILOW TUNE.

MANILOW, EH? LEMME CHECK OUR PLAYLIST... HMM... HMM... HOLD IT. HERE'S ONE:

"HARI-KARI FOR BARRY"

OH, IS THAT ONE OF HIS?

MR. DALLAS... I HEAR SOME ROCK PERFORMERS BITE THE HEADS OFF BATS! DO YOU GUYS... YA KNOW... DO THAT SORT OF THING?

YOUNGBLATT, IF YOU DON'T STOP BUGGING ME, I'LL HAVE MY LEAD TONGUE-PLAYER BITE THE HEAD OFF YOUR WIFE.

OH MY.

OPUS... TRY YOUR WA-WA PEDAL NOW. ANYTHING?

NOPE.

DRAT!

MR. DALLAS... WERE YOU SINCERE WITH THAT OFFER?

♪ SATAN DON'T GIVE ME DEM PIMPLES.. ♪ PIMPLES-OH! PIMPLES-OH! PIMPLES FROM HELL

TAKE IT —BILL!

BILL, WHAT DID I TELL YOU ABOUT DISCOURAGING GROUPIES...

I'M YOURS.

OH, FOR GOD'S SAKE, BARBARA..

PARDON ME. THIS ISN'T WHERE THE BAND PARTY IS, IS IT?

THEY INVITED A FEW OF US UP TO THEIR SUITE AFTER THE BANQUET.

THE LEAD TONGUE-PLAYER SAID WE WOULD BE TESTING EINSTEIN'S THEORY OF "GLIDING HOTEL FURNITURE."

GRRRR..

ARE YOU FAMILIAR WITH THAT THEORY?

WHAT'S GOING ON IN THERE, BLOB-BUTT?

BILL THE CAT IS THROWING A PARTY.

WE INVITED UP A FEW OF THE MOOSE WIVES' AUXILIARY... MY, THEY'RE A LIVELY BUNCH!

ALTHOUGH, TO BE HONEST, THINGS ARE BEGINNING TO GET A LITTLE OUT OF HAND.

WHAT ARE YOU WEARING?

A WALLPAPER TOGA. BILL FLUSHED THE SHEETS DOWN THE TOILET BACK AROUND 1:30.

AWRIGHT, EVERYBODY... SETTLE DOWN... PARTY'S OVER!

LADIES.. PLEASE COLLECT YOUR THINGS... HODGE-PODGE, GET OFF THE LAMP AND PUT OUT THE FIRE IN THE REFRIGERATOR.

BILL! PUT ALL THAT DOWN! BILL... GET AWAY FROM THE WINDOW...

DISPATCH... GIVE ME THAT ROOM NUMBER AGAIN.

DINETTE SET CLOSING IN AT 12 O'CLOCK...

POLIC

EVERYBODY FREEZE! WHO'S RESPONSIBLE FOR THIS MOTEL MAYHEM?

I TRIED TO STOP THEM, OFFICER.

THEM? A BIRD, A RABBIT AND A CAT THREW ALL THE FURNITURE OUT THE WINDOW?

THEY HAD TOO MUCH ROOT BEER.

RIGHT. I SUPPOSE THEY CAN TALK, TOO.

OF COURSE THEY CAN TALK. THEY CAN SING "PIMPLES FROM HELL" IN FOUR DIFFERENT KEYS!!

RIGHT. AND I GOT A CAMEL THAT CAN YODEL IN FIVE.

WOULD YOU GUYS JUST SAY SOMETHING. ANYTHING.

MEOW.

AGAINST THE WALL, NUT-BRAIN. THIS AIN'T THE FUNNY PAGES.

YER GONNA DIE! DID YA HEAR ME?! DIE! DIE! DIE!!

CHIRP. I SAY, CHIRP.

OPUS HAD BEEN WALKING IN THE WOODS HUMMING A RECENT WAYNE NEWTON HIT, AS MANY OF US DO, WHEN THE WHOLE TERRIBLE, DARK TRUTH SMACKED HIM IN THE PUSS LIKE A CUSTARD PIE...

YEEAIGH!

WHAT?! WHATSA MATTER?! COMMUNISTS?

SUDDENLY IT JUST CAME TO ME! THE SHOCKING REALIZATION THAT...THAT I'M AS HANDSOME AS I'M GONNA GET... AND THAT'S NOT TOO HANDSOME!

I'VE ALWAYS ALLOWED MYSELF THE NOTION THAT I WILL SOMEHOW, SOMEDAY, IMPROVE...THAT I'LL GROW INTO MY HONKER!...SPROUT A CHIN! GET SVELTE!... GROW A PAIR OF CUTE LEGS! BUT I JUST HIT PENGUIN MIDDLE AGE!!...

...DEVELOPMENTALLY SPEAKING, I'VE REACHED THE TOP OF MY MOUNTAIN... BUT IT'S JUST A MOLEHILL!

SOMEONE CALL AN AMBULANCE!

SOMEONE DID, AND THEY TOOK HOME A HYSTERICAL OPUS CONCERNED ABOUT HIS FUTURE...

WRINKLES! WRINKLES! WRINKLES!

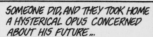

SIX PINTS OF "OIL OF OLAY" BEAUTY LOTION WERE PURCHASED AND LIBERALLY APPLIED TO THE PATIENT...

GLOP!

...WHO WAS THEN PUT TO BED, WHERE HE STUCK TO THE SHEETS. EVENTUALLY, HE WAS REMOVED LIKE A MUSHED BANANA FROM "SARAN WRAP," RINSED AND JUDGED STILL TO BE LIGHT YEARS AWAY IN LOOKS FROM MEL GIBSON.

LIFE, HOWEVER, WENT ON...AS DID OPUS, WHO PLEDGED NEVER AGAIN TO HUM WAYNE NEWTON SONGS IN THE WOODS.